By M. L. Bullock

Chapter One—Roger Southland

I sat in the opulent dining room, bathed in the warm glow of a crystal chandelier overhead. The flickering candlelight, encased in ornate, golden sconces, cast dancing shadows across the faces of the men gathered around the table. The walls were adorned with rich, dark wood paneling, intricately carved with scenes of hunting and grandeur. The aroma of expensive cigars filled the air, mingling with the faint scent of aged oak and polished leather. This was surely the finest home this side of the Mississippi.

How dare Barney Dooley think he deserved such a home? He was a nobody. A man who got lucky and married a rich orphan who was as meek as a spooked church mouse.

There were five of us at the poker table, but the only face worth noting was that of Barney Dooley. A man I hated and considered my mortal enemy.

He was the owner of the plantation that sprawled across five hundred acres of fertile land—land that would soon be mine. Barney sat at the head of the table, in an intricately carved mahogany chair, its deep red velvet upholstery matching the plush draperies that framed the grand windows. He puffed on his oversized cigar, coughing as he attempted to appear as a sophisticate. One who knew how to smoke. It was clear he was not.

"Your move, Southland," Barney sneered, his eyes narrowed like a snake sizing up its prey. The room, filled with the trappings of wealth and power, was a testament to his undeserved luck. He was oblivious to the reality that he was the prey, and I was the hunter, armed with more than just a winning hand.

I didn't just want to win this house, I wanted to destroy him.

Clara, my lover, and my servant, hovered behind me as Barney leered at her. I tilted my head slightly but did not look directly at her or him. She would know to avoid his gaze. She should be used to stupid men's ogling expressions. She would know how to behave. Clara would not shift around or move awkwardly. My lover would remember my constant instructions, "Be quiet and do as I do."

I reached a hand up and she put her soft hand on my shoulder.

Yes, she was firmly under my control. Let Barney stare at her all he wanted.

He would never know the pleasure of touching such a perfect feminine specimen. She was elegance perfected. No, he would never have a woman as lovely as Clara. Barney Dooley had saddled himself with the plainest woman in the South. Unfortunately, she was also one of the wealthiest.

I singularly hated Barney Dooley and I wasn't sure why. I could not put my finger on the moment I knew he was my mortal enemy. How long had I hated him? I could not really say. It was almost as if it had always been like this.

The hatred between Dooley and I had created fodder for more than one newspaper article, and more than one court case. I once went into business with the fool and summarily lost a considerable amount of money, but I got it all back. There would be no more deals with Dooley. I was no longer toying with him.

Tonight, that all would end. Finally, the best man would win. I always did.

I glanced at my cards and then at the pile of money, the deed, and the trinkets that made up the pot. The table itself was a masterpiece, its dark wood inlaid with intricate patterns of ivory. All eyes were on me, waiting, watching. Oh, how I reveled in the tension. I couldn't help but flash my signature grin, the one that unsettled even the most seasoned poker players.

I was born for moments like these. It had taken months, years even, to push this fool into this game, and now I had him in my sights. Dead to rights he was.

"All in," I declared with a flourish, shoving my entire stack of chips into the center of the table, my eyes locked onto Barney's. The chips, crafted from ivory and meticulously engraved with delicate patterns of vines and leaves, clinked together like a symphony of wealth.

It was a moment suspended in time, a high-stakes gamble amidst the opulent backdrop of the plantation's grand dining room. I heard Clara's soft gasp behind me. I would punish her for that later, in my own way. She'd been instructed to remain quiet.

Clara poured me another glass of wine as I waited for Barney's shock to dissipate. She served me elegantly, carefully revealing her slender wrists as she did so. I knew the other men would be jealous of my having such beauty by my side.

Let them see that lovely skin of hers. That would be all of Clara's skin they would ever see. Clara was forever mine.

A chorus of gasps and hushed whispers rippled through the onlookers, their eyes torn between my audacity and the fear of what would come next. I reveled in their discomfort, for I had orchestrated this game meticulously, and victory was a foregone conclusion.

Barney's eyes widened for just a second, a fleeting moment of doubt that betrayed him. At that moment, I knew I had him. He had been foolish enough to bet his plantation—his legacy—against me, Roger Southland.

"Damn," he finally said, his voice trembling beneath the veneer of composure, his gaze never leaving mine.

As the cards were revealed, a victorious laugh escaped my lips, a sound that echoed through the room's lavish surroundings. I had done it. I had won. The Dooley Plantation was mine, and Barney Dooley had sealed his fate. My eyes met his one last time before I collected my new deed and all his cash.

"Oh, Barney," I mused, savoring the sweet taste of triumph. "You should know by now; I don't like to be beaten. Collect our winnings, Clara." My lover revealed a red velvet bag and prepared to fill it with my winnings.

Barney began to sputter. "This isn't over, you bastard! Southland, you ain't ever going to own my place. Never!"

I laughed in his face. As the last of the chips clinked on the table, the room fell into a hushed silence. Nobody else had much to say.

The opulent surroundings seemed to close in, suffocatingly as if the very walls were privy to the gravity of the moment. A chill settled in the air, and I couldn't help but feel it, a shiver that danced down my spine, whispering of the impending consequences.

"You dare renege on your bet, Barney Dooley? Is that what you're saying?"

"I'll make sure you get what you want, Southland. You'll get what you want!" Barney Dooley rose from the table, his chair clattered as he stomped out of the room. Barney's parting words, dripping with bitterness, clung to the opulent surroundings like a haunting specter. The legacy of his grand estate was now in my hands, but what price had I truly paid to claim it?

My inner voice, that nagging whisper of doubt, grew louder, questioning the cost of my relentless ambition. *What strange thoughts, Southland! You won! You are the victor! In one card game, you have destroyed your enemy!*

One by one, the other men departed, casting backward glances at me, glances filled with a blend of respect and apprehension. They were merely spectators in my grand play, and their opinions mattered little.

Clara kissed my cheek obediently.

When the last of them had gone, I took a deep breath, allowing the reality of the situation to sink in. This was mine now, all of it. But before I grew too comfortable in my newfound wealth, there was one final matter to attend to. I nodded at Clara after I kissed her passionately. I took the title in my own hands.

I wasn't done with Dooley.

I hurried out of the plantation and strode across the expansive lawn, where I found Barney, pacing furiously back and forth. His plain face was marred by defeat. I noticed the dampness on his cheeks, but it did not stir any sympathy within me. I had none, for what it was worth. He was a man who didn't belong, a man who had merely ridden the wave of fortune for a short while, only to have it crash against him.

"Dooley," I said, brandishing the deed in my hand like a cruel trophy. "You and your family have until sunset tomorrow to vacate this property. I suggest you use your time wisely. Not out here crying or cursing the heavens. You lost in a fair game, Dooley."

He looked up, his eyes bloodshot, a whirlwind of rage and humiliation swirling within them. "Fair game?" He chuckled, a bitter sound that echoed through the night. "You may have won the land,

Southland, but you've lost your soul in the process. Remember, not everything can be bought."

"I don't want to own everything, Dooley. And I have no use for your soul but I do own your place," I declared, waving the deed one last time, my voice dripping with arrogance. "I mean, my place. And that's all that matters."

His hands clenched into fists. I half expected him to swing on me, but he did not. I didn't blame him, although I was the victor, there was a strange air about this place tonight.

I'd never noticed it before, but it wasn't enough to put me off the scent. Almost.

As I walked back to fetch my coat and horse— and my woman, the words of my defeated rival gnawed at the edges of my conscience.

Barney's warning lingered like a dark cloud, threatening to unleash a tempest of regret. But I pushed it away, locking it deep within. In a life where the stakes were always high, I had just hit the jackpot.

Or so I believed. I paused as I climbed in the carriage. A chill settled deep into my body. The arm lights of the nearby tavern glittered welcomingly. Clara smiled at me proudly. I had every intention to take leave her at home while I celebrated my victory. There would be time to punish her later.

No need to run home. No need to worry over anything. A celebratory drink is in order.

Hours later, I was making my way out of the dimly lit tavern when Barney Dooley, whose eyes were heavy with defeat and something darker, something ominous, caught up with me. He grabbed my arm, his fingers clawing into my coat like talons.

"Southland," he rasped, his voice thick with a desperation I'd never heard before. "You've got to listen to me."

"Get away from me, you bastard! You lost fair and square!" My words slurred as I spoke my warning.

Barney Dooley would not be deterred. "That house, it isn't just a house. It wants something from everyone. It wants something from me, it'll want something from you. It'll demand blood."

I scoffed at him, wrenching my arm away. "What's the matter, Dooley? Having second thoughts about the hand you've played? It's a little late for that." My head felt a bit light and it wouldn't take much for the scrawny, thin man to overcome me, if I were being honest. But I would never tell him that.

"It's not about the game or the cards, Roger," he snapped, his eyes searching mine, feverish. "It's about the hands that built that place, and the souls that have been lost within its walls. The bloody land it was built on! You idiot! Why would you want that house?"

"Go home and pack, Barney. I have no further desire to discuss this with you. If you're not out tomorrow, I will show up with the marshal."

Barney sputtered, "You're forcing me to do evil. You cannot understand! Please believe me! Their blood will be on you."

"Evil?" I sneered, the taste of victory still fresh on my lips. "This is about honor and the consequences of risk. You gambled, you lost, and now you're looking for an escape."

"No," he shot back, his voice trembling. "I'm looking to spare you from an evil I've known far too long. An evil that'll haunt your days and plague your nights. You only see a grand home. What lies beneath is real and angry and it will not spare you!"

My laugh was loud and bitter. "Is that your last play, Barney? Ghost stories to frighten me out of my winnings?" The idea that the man was so desperate to dissuade me that he'd try to frighten me with ghost stories tickled me to no end. What a fool!

"Mark my words," Barney said, his eyes locking onto mine with an intensity that sent a chill down my spine. "That house will exact its price, Roger. You can change its name, I don't care. I have already heard that you will but it won't matter. The spirits, the ones that dwell there, they have a name, an evil name. And when they come for you, remember this night. Remember that I warned you."

With that, he turned and stumbled out of the tavern, his steps heavy with the weight of unspeakable fears. I shook my head, dismissing his words as the drunken ramblings of a sore loser.

"Go home, fool," I muttered under my breath, folding up the deed to my new home and tucking it into my coat pocket. "Go tell your wife what a loser you are, Barney. The deal is done."

Little did I know, as I stepped out into the crisp night air, that Barney Dooley's warning would echo in the halls of the strange mansion for years to come.

It was a prophecy written in shadows and sealed with a foreboding I was too arrogant to understand.

Chapter Two—Roger

I awoke the next morning, the sun filtering through the curtains of my rented room, casting a warm glow on the ornate wallpaper. Despite the odd sense of foreboding that had tinged last night's events, I couldn't help but feel invincible. After all, luck had been my lady, and she'd given me the Dooley Plantation.

I dressed myself, pocketing the deed once again as if it were a talisman—a piece of magic that could only bring fortune and prosperity.

Clara left earlier to begin packing and moving all my belongings. I'd sent for her last night and she'd come to me without fuss or complaint. *Such a compliant woman. How I delighted in her.* I would not waste any time taking possession of the plantation and I meant what I said. I was going to move into the Dooley place right away. It would no longer be called the Dooley Plantation, but Southland.

Honestly, I could not imagine going to the home I'd once shared with Rebecca ever again. I wanted that part of my life banished forever. Funny to think how in love I'd once been. How human I'd been. No more. I had Clara to serve my needs and I did not love her, nor was I going to. One did not marry a servant and I needn't fool myself. She certainly did not love me either.

I was a man of action, I smiled to myself. I'd proven it yesterday and would continue to do so.

As I descended the stairs of the hotel, I found myself humming a tune, a soft melody that seemed to capture the essence of my newfound confidence. My steps were light, my demeanor radiant. I had every reason to believe that fate was on my side.

Walking into the dining room for a morning coffee, I expected the usual nods of recognition, perhaps even a few congratulatory slaps on the back. But what greeted me was a suffocating silence, a stillness that was immediately disquieting.

The waitress, usually chatty and cheerful, barely looked at me as she poured my coffee. Her hand trembled, causing a few drops to splash onto the saucer.

"Is everything alright?" I finally asked, breaking the silence. Her eyes met mine, filled with a mixture of pity and something else. Fear, perhaps, or maybe just disbelief.

"You haven't heard, then? I guess you wouldn't have, seeing as how you just came down. It's terrible, sir."

"Heard what?" The coffee cup paused midway to my lips.

"It's Barney Dooley, Mr. Southland. He's dead. All of 'em are dead."

The cup clattered back onto the saucer, sending ripples through the coffee. "Dead? How?"

"Killed himself, they're saying. Found him shot dead at the entrance of his home. The whole family gone too. Darn shame."

My mind raced, the walls of the café seeming to close in on me. Barney's eyes, alight with that indescribable fire, flashed before me. His words—a threat or a warning—echoed in my ears.

Their blood will be on your hands.

And in that moment, I felt it—a fracture in my reality, a small but undeniable crack in my shield of luck and invincibility. Yet, even as the news of

Barney's tragic end washed over me, I still felt that same sense of destiny.

Was it arrogance, or just the intoxication of my newfound wealth and power? I couldn't say.

What I did know was that I was still the owner of Dooley Plantation, still the man who'd bested Barney in the ultimate game of chance and skill. But at what cost?

I left the hotel café without finishing my coffee. The deed to Dooley Plantation weighed heavy in my pocket, now a millstone rather than a talisman. As I walked through the town square, people averted their eyes, whispers filled the air, and for the first time, I questioned whether my luck was a blessing or a curse.

But even in that moment of introspection, a stubborn voice within me resisted the doubt and clung to the belief that I was Roger Southland, master of my own fate.

The game had consequences, but it was a game I had won. And I was convinced, perhaps foolishly, that luck would continue to favor me, that the roll of the dice or the turn of the cards would bring me nothing but aces and eights.

I had yet to realize that in the grand tapestry of Southland and Dooley, aces and eights were known as the Dead Man's Hand.

As I walked away from the café, the news of Barney's death seemed to hang in the air like an acrid fog. Each step I took felt like a move in a chess game, the board laid out on a battlefield I didn't fully understand. It was as if Barney had made one last play, a fatal gambit that changed the stakes yet again.

A sense of unreality gripped me. Just yesterday, Barney and I had been adversaries across a brightly lit table, and now he was gone—his life snuffed out. It was unthinkable.

What happened? Did I really need to ask? Did I really need to wonder? I knew the answer although I didn't dare verbalize it.

A chill crept up my spine, but it wasn't just the morning air that made me shudder.
Still, intermingled with my shock was a hardened resolve. I'd won the Dooley plantation fair and square. No shadow cast by tragedy, however dark, could or should take it from me.

I found myself wrestling with this grim determination as I reached the lawyer's office to formalize my claim on the Dooley Plantation.

"Ah, Mr. Southland. I assume you've heard the news?" Mr. Thompson, the family lawyer for generations of Dooleys, greeted me with a gravitas that belied his usually affable demeanor. "Cal Harvey told me about the deed transfer. I expect you'll be wanting to settle that, after the funeral of course"

"I only just heard the news," was all I could muster. My voice sounded distant, detached, as if the words were being spoken by someone else. "He must have been a mad man."

"Terrible, terrible business. The Dooley family has a long and storied history, but this... this is a sorrowful chapter, indeed."

I nodded, taking a seat across from his imposing oak desk. "About the deed—I really don't want to wait, Mr. Thompson."

Mr. Thompson eyed me for a moment before speaking, as if assessing my worthiness to be the new steward of the Dooley legacy. "All in good time, Mr. Southland. But you must understand that your, ahem, acquisition of the estate has raised a few eyebrows, to say the least. It wouldn't be right to do this today. It's too terrible. Terrible for everyone."

"I won the deed—and the house and all the land. It's mine by law. That was a fair game. No one can say otherwise. It must be done today."

The lawyer sighed. "Cal Harvey was adamant that you won it honestly. Said you appeared to be the luckiest man alive, but it was all above board. All an honest gamble. But truth be told, the winning can't help but have a little taint to it. The church social group probably won't be visiting your new place. Well, as you're here already we better get the dirty business over with."

As the lawyer started pulling out the necessary papers, my mind began to wander. Barney's eyes, filled with a tempest of emotions, looked at me from the depths of my memory. Despite my resolve, doubt began to creep into the corners of my thoughts. Dirty business? There had been nothing dirty about that game. What had I really won? A bad reputation.

We went through the formalities, and soon enough, the deed was transferred. I was the official owner of Dooley Plantation, but the victory was bittersweet. The house I'd won, the land it sat on, the ancient oak trees—they all felt like hollow prizes now. Yet, my determination remained.

I was Roger Southland, and luck was my birthright, even if it now felt tainted.

"May I offer some advice?" Mr. Thompson said, breaking my reverie as he handed me the finalized deed.

"Go ahead."

"Be careful, Mr. Southland. Houses like the Dooley Plantation have memories. They absorb the joys and tragedies of those who've lived there. And sometimes, they have a way of—how should I put this—settling accounts. I understand men like you. Men with a mind for money and possessions, but there are things beyond that, sir."

"What things might that be, sir?" I asked without pretending to be interested in his answer.

"Matters of decency, Mr. Southland. This could have waited. A week or two. The man is dead and to make matters worse, he took his whole family with him. Now, I cannot say you drove him to that madness, but others might."

I met his gaze, his words echoing in the same chamber of my mind where Barney's final words resided. I gripped the deed tighter. "Why would they say that? What did he do to his family?"

"He murdered them, Mr. Southland. Barney Dooley stabbed his two children and shot his wife. The whole family is dead and I'd be surprised if they've even had a chance to clean up the blood yet. As I said, these things take time."

I went as white as a sheet. I knew this because I could see my face in the mirror across from Mr. Thompson's desk. It was a shaving mirror no doubt, for days when men like Thompson would spend far too many hours in his office.

I offered no rebuke. No commentary. I took my paperwork and left the lawyer's office, my steps heavy yet unyielding. My mind was reeling with this insanity. No, the fate of the Dooley family wasn't my fault. A coward like Barney Dooley, he was the kind of man that would do something awful like that.

"Not my fault!" I growled to myself as I walked back to the hotel to fetch my things. No. I wasn't going to do that. I'd let Clara send someone after my odds and ends. I had to go to the plantation.

The stakes had been raised—Dooley had raised them from beyond the grave and whatever hand I'd been dealt, I was all in.

I had no choice in the matter. I retrieved my horse and rode for the property I'd won. It wasn't my first time visiting the place, but this was the first time I'd come as the owner.

My first steps onto the Dooley Plantation as its rightful owner were a strange blend of triumph, revulsion, and apprehension.

The large manor loomed before me, a grand structure of dark wood and weathered stone. Once a symbol of prosperity and southern grandeur, it now appeared as a forlorn relic, worn down by the elements and the weight of its own history.

Others were here. I recognized the marshal and his deputy. They didn't appear to be happy to see me, but what could they do? I owned the place. Fair and square. I patted the deed in my pocket, more to comfort myself than show the marshal my legal right of ownership.

The ancient oak tree that stood near the entrance like a silent sentinel seemed overly large today. The morning light filtered through the abundant green leaves.

As I approached it, a sudden gust of wind rustled its leaves, causing them to murmur softly as if whispering a warning—or perhaps a welcome, I couldn't be sure.

At least Barney's body had been covered and moved from the doorway. As I walked in, the smell of blood and fear met me.

The inside of the house felt like a time capsule; everything was exactly as I remembered from the times I had visited as a guest—fine antique furniture, ornate chandeliers, intricate wallpaper peeling slightly at the edges. But last night, it had seemed richer. It had appeared a greater treasure. Here in the light of day, the plantation gave a different feel. One I could not describe.

"Sir, would you mind stepping out of the house? We haven't had time to retrieve Mrs. Dooley or the children yet. Here comes the wagon though."

The new marshal, whose name escaped me shook his head in disgust. His disgust better be for the dead man, the coward that annihilated his whole family and not me.

"This is my property, marshal. I'll go look around if you don't mind. I wouldn't want any of my property to come up missing."

"Why would you want to do that? Haven't you caused enough heartache for one day? Hell, make that a lifetime? Show some respect, Southland. If you have any."

I ignored his disapproval and ascended the grand staircase, each carpeted step creaking under my weight as if groaning in protest, or perhaps recognition. When I reached the top, I found myself instinctively drawn to what used to be Barney's study. That's where her tiny body lay, the late Mrs. Dooley. A plain, pale woman painted red with the gunshot positioned between her eyes.

Oh yes. Her eyes were wide open and staring at me. As if she were accusing me.

Without warning I gagged, almost wretched, but I managed to swallow the bile. But I had to keep going. I had to see what he'd done. Or maybe I'd done. I would never admit that to anyone else but I was beginning to see my own hand in this tragedy. I had to witness the carnage.

Why? Why did I need to see the children too?

As I pushed the nearby door open, it squeaked eerily on its hinges. Instinctively, I knew it was a bedroom.

That's when I heard it—a soft, almost inaudible whisper, like the rustling of the oak leaves outside, but coming from within the house. I strained my ears to listen, but just as quickly as it had started, the sound vanished into silence.

It would have been easy to attribute it to my imagination, to the rush of emotions and events that had led me to this moment. Yet, deep down, I knew that it was something more, something that defied rational explanation. Barney's words echoed in my mind,

"You haven't won anything yet, Roger."

I could not see him, but I heard him. And I saw the two children, piled on top of one another. A boy and a girl, both tow-headed, but now red.

Red all over. A long silver blade lay beside them. I wanted to scream, scream at the top of my lungs. I couldn't do it. I couldn't speak at all.

Stepping back from the room, I couldn't shake the feeling that the house was alive in some way, that it was aware of my presence—and of my victory. And in that disquieting moment, the walls of the Dooley Plantation seemed to close in ever so slightly, as if to say that the house had accepted a new owner, but the game was far from over.

With a sense of both dread and anticipation, I realized that while I might have won the deed to this grand, haunted place, earning my right to truly call it home was a different battle altogether—a battle that I was only just beginning to understand.

It was Dooley who had gone all in.

All into hell.

Chapter Three—Roger

The move-in day arrived with a cloudless sky, the sun cast its golden glow over the vast estate. Clara directed the movers as they hauled furniture and boxes inside the grand manor. Honestly, the massive home was already loaded to the brim with fine furniture.

Sam and Jenny, our gardener and cook respectively, were also bustling around, doing their best to make Southland mine.

I made the formal changes, legally establishing the former Dooley Plantation as Southland. I expected my wishes to be respected by my staff and anyone visiting the place. It would forever be known as Southland.

I would banish the memory of Barney Dooley and his foul deeds from my memory—from the collective memory too. He thought he would put me off taking possession by performing such a heinous act. Barney Dooley hadn't understood who he was playing with.

"Mr. Southland wants the antique mirror there, Sam," Clara called out to the wiry gardener. Her voice had a sharpness that could cut through any indecision, a trait that had served me well over the years. She would never use that tone of voice on me, but I expected her to deploy it on the help.

Clara had been my lover since the day I buried Rebecca. She'd been Rebecca's companion, her friend but for the fact that she was mixed race, she would have plenty of options. Many young men would have come to call. But alas for her, no white man would dare to marry her.

Their stupidity for Clara was quite the catch.

I had always found her attractive, but compared to Rebecca, she'd been a faded flower. My Rebecca had been a rose, perfect and lovely. Clara had an attractive earthiness, plump breasts and eyes that changed colors. A rare trait that betrayed her moods.

"On second thought, place it in the hallway, Clara," I instructed, watching as Sam and two hired movers gingerly carried the heavy, ornate mirror adorned with intricate gold leaf designs.

The house seemed to watch me, its wooden floors creaking under the weight of new occupants and foreign furniture. I had been living alone since Rebecca's death, or almost alone, and the idea of filling this huge mansion with people and activity was both comforting and oddly intrusive. It was as if we were disturbing something. Or someone.

Listen to you, Roger. Such ridiculous thoughts. You're as jumpy as Clara and Jenny.

Once the move was well underway, I decided to escape the organized chaos and take a stroll through the property. Sam had left the house and went into the garden to work a bit. He'd said something about planting new blooms, Rebecca's blooms. She'd been quite the fan of roses. Rather an amateur botanist.

Planting roses. What a joke. As if I were trying to counterbalance the dark history of the place with a new, vibrant life.

I reminded him that the vegetable garden needed attention, more attention that my late wife's transplanted roses. *Forgive me, Rebecca. I cannot think of you often. Your memory stirs my heart, my cold, dead heart.*

As I walked back inside, I toured the mansion once more. I ignored the creaks of the walls and the pops of the floors beneath me.

Don't want you here. Get out. Don't want you here!

I stood poised on the grand staircase unsure whether to believe my own ears. No, I hadn't heard Dooley's voice, but I sensed it.

Thankfully, Clara summoned me downstairs as she held a stack of mail that had arrived. "Sir, you might want to look at this," she said, handing me an old, tattered envelope without a return address. My name was written in a shaky hand, and my curiosity piqued. "It appears to be another one."

With a grimace I tore open the cheap envelope. Inside, a single note read: "You don't belong there. Leave before they come!"

I looked at Clara, her eyes narrowing as if trying to read my reaction. "Do you know anything about this?"

"No. How would I? A sick joke is all."

An unsettling feeling washed over me. Was this a prank, or something more? I couldn't be sure, but the message felt like it echoed the sentiments of the very walls around us.

"We'll find out soon enough," I murmured, almost to myself. "I will go see the marshal later today."

As the day wore on and the sun began its descent, casting long, creeping shadows across the rooms, I felt a tingling sense of apprehension.

It wasn't just the haunting beauty of the descending darkness, or the stillness that came with it—it was a sense that we were not alone, that our every move was being watched, calculated, and weighed.

And as the last of the boxes were unpacked, and my new life in my hard-won home began to take shape, the feeling became a conviction.

I wasn't just the new owner of Southland Plantation. I was the latest player in a game that had been played for generations, with rules I was only beginning to understand.

The first week at the Southland Plantation passed with an undercurrent of eerie stillness. At first, I attributed it to the natural adjustment period—new place, new people, new routines. But then things began happening that I couldn't quite dismiss as figments of my overactive imagination.

It started with the lights. Old houses often have quirks, so when the chandelier in the dining room swung erratically during our first dinner, I thought little of it. But when it happened again—and then again, and only during moments when the conversation turned to the house's history or Barney's tragic end—I felt a knot of unease tighten within me.

"There must be a draft, Mr. Southland," Clara offered one evening, staring at the twisting chandelier as if it were a puzzle to solve.

The chandelier could have been written off as drafts, but the sounds that began to fill the house in the dead of night were harder to ignore.

Soft whispers floated down the empty hallways, always just at the edge of hearing, unintelligible but deeply unsettling. Louder moans and groans echoed through the halls too.

I would often find myself waking up in the middle of the night, the sensation of being watched clinging to me like a cold, wet blanket.

Then came the shadows.

They were always just out of focus, flitting around corners and vanishing when I turned to look directly at them. They never appeared when others were around, only showed themselves when I was alone, making me question whether I was seeing things—or losing my mind.

Each incident, taken alone, seemed like a trifle. But together, they wove a tapestry of dread that clung to me, growing thicker with each passing day. I couldn't talk openly about it without sounding like a superstitious fool, yet the sense that I was not alone—had never been alone— since moving in, was overpowering.

One particularly chilling evening, while sipping whiskey in what used to be Barney's study, I glanced towards the window. For a brief second, I saw a shadowy figure standing outside, looking in. My heart leaped into my throat, and I rushed to the window only to find...nothing. The lawn stretched empty in the moonlight, not a soul in sight. And how would anyone be standing there?

The smaller study, Barney's private study was on the second floor.

I stood there for a moment, grappling with the growing fear that perhaps winning this house was not a victory, but a sentence.

A slight breeze swept through the room even though the window was closed, rustling the old pages of Barney's books that still adorned the bookshelves.

I took a deep breath to steady myself. "I won you fair and square," I whispered, as much to myself as to the lingering spirit of Barney Dooley, or whatever else occupied this house with me.

As if in response, the room fell into darkness, the candles flickering out for a heartbeat before lighting again. And I knew, beyond a shadow of a doubt, that my claim over the Southland was anything but settled.

Night had fully settled over Southland, and the dread I'd felt all week had reached an acute sense of impending doom. I couldn't place it, couldn't give it form—it was a shadowy whisper, a cold wind, an electric charge in the air.

I went to bed that night with the candles burning in hopes that the candlelight would be a barricade against the darkness and whatever it hid. But sleep remained elusive, each creak of the floorboards or rustle of leaves outside my window causing my eyes to snap open and my body to tense.

And then, as if to mock my feeble attempts at security, all the candles blew out at once. Someone invisible blew them out. I heard a deep, long breath. I suddenly wished I had insisted that Clara stay with me.

The room was plunged into a deep, impenetrable darkness. My breathing became shallow and fast; my heartbeat drummed loudly in my ears. Straining to listen, I thought

I heard the faintest of whispers, like a distant conversation happening in a language I couldn't understand.

"Get a grip, Roger," I muttered to myself. "It's an old house. Old houses make sounds."

I was just about to rise and fetch fresh candles when it happened: the soft, unmistakable sound of footsteps. They started at the far end of the hallway, growing louder and steadier as they approached my bedroom door.

My skin crawled; my muscles froze. The steps came to a halt just outside my door, and then— the knocks. Three slow, deliberate taps.

Tap, tap, tap!

I bolted from the bed, tripping over my own feet in my haste. My hand fumbled around in the dark, finally finding the doorknob. I yanked the door open. Nothing. The hallway was a pitch-black void.

"Clara! Where are you? Is that you?"

Clara's soft voice did not answer me. Another voice whispered to me. It was scratchy and intelligible.

It was too much. Reason, courage, skepticism— everything was drowned out by an overpowering urge to escape. I opened the door and then like a coward, I turned and ran, my feet pounding down the staircase, my hands outstretched in the suffocating darkness.

Something was inside that room!

I burst through the front door, gasping for air as if I'd been submerged underwater. The night was alive around me, but I couldn't appreciate its beauty, couldn't hear the crickets, or feel the cool wind on my skin.

All I felt was terror—a primal, all-consuming terror.

My eyes darted around the porch and front yard, half-expecting to see some malevolent figure lurking in the moonlight. But I was utterly alone. Or so it seemed.

As I stood there, trembling, I heard it—a guttural growl, so low and so close it could have been a part of the wind. It seemed to come from everywhere and nowhere, filling the night, filling my soul.

And in that moment, I realized I wasn't just a man standing outside his house. I was prey.

My instincts screamed at me to run—to leave this cursed ground and never look back. I took one step, then another, my bare feet crushing the gravel path that led away from the house. Each step felt like a small victory, a reclaiming of my sanity from the shadowy grip that had taken hold of me.

Just when I thought I had put enough distance between myself and the haunting walls of the former Dooley Plantation, I heard it—the creaking of a door swinging open. The sound pierced the silence of the night like a knife, turning my blood to ice.

My eyes, wide with fear, darted back to the house. Through the darkness, I could barely make out the front door. It stood wide open as if inviting me back into the arms of my nightmares.

Then a voice broke through the silence, a voice so familiar it sent chills down my spine.

"Roger, is that you?" It was Clara, her tone tinged with confusion that couldn't match the terror engulfing me.

For a moment, I was torn.

Part of me wanted to sprint back to the house, to make sure Clara and the others were safe. Another part, a much larger part, whispered insidiously that this was another trap, another twisted game played by the malevolent forces that occupied the house. Was that truly my lover seeking me?

"Roger!" Clara's voice was tinged with panic now. "Where are you?"

That was enough to break my paralysis. Whatever haunted that house, whatever malicious entity lurked in its shadowy corners, it wouldn't take them—not if I could help it. Ignoring every screaming instinct, I turned and ran back toward the house, my heart pounding in my chest, my fear giving way to a grim determination.

I bounded up the steps, through the open door, and into the yawning darkness of the house. "Clara! Where are you?" I shouted, my voice reverberating through the empty halls.

Then, without warning, all the candles flickered back on. All the candles and lamps in every downstairs room. I blinked, momentarily blinded by the sudden brightness. As my eyes adjusted, I looked around and found myself alone—utterly, inexplicably alone.

"Clara?" I called out again, my voice tinged with a dread I couldn't shake. There was no response, not even the faintest echo of my own voice.

And as I stood there, in the eerily silent house, a sinking feeling settled into the pit of my stomach. Something was horribly wrong. Something had shifted, irrevocably, turning the house from a mere building of bricks and wood into a living, breathing entity that wanted something from me.

What that something was, I couldn't say.

As I stood alone in what should have been my triumphant prize, a haunting realization washed over me: I had gotten into a game far more dangerous, and far more ancient, than a simple hand of poker.

And the stakes were higher than I could have ever imagined.

As the ticking of the grandfather clock reached a fevered pitch, a sudden gust of wind howled through the house, extinguishing all the lights again. I was plunged back into an unsettling darkness. The blackness around me seemed to deepen, to thicken, becoming almost palpable.

My heart pounded in my chest as I fumbled for a nearby matchbox.

Before I could strike it, a whisper slithered through the air, a voice neither entirely human nor entirely... anything else I could identify. "Roger Southland," it hissed, echoing in the corners of the room as if spoken by the walls themselves.

I froze, the matchstick trembling in my hand.

"Your voice," the whisper continued, "will serve as a fine instrument. You have no innocence. You have nothing else to offer, I will accept it. For now."

Before I could react, a shadow detached itself from the corner of the room and lunged at me. It engulfed me whole, wrapping around me like a second skin. My mouth opened to scream, but no sound came out. I felt a hand shoved into my throat which was followed by a tremendous unyielding pain.

I could not scream. I could not protest. Only hope to live and breathe again. My voice was trapped, stolen by whatever malevolent force inhabited this cursed place.

And then, as suddenly as it had appeared, the shadow receded. The candles flickered back to life, their flames dancing as if mocking my newfound muteness. My voice was gone, absorbed by the entity that haunted this house—this prison.

I rushed to a mirror and peered at my reflection. My eyes met eyes that weren't entirely my own anymore—they were darker, somehow, as if a part of my very soul had been sucked away. I opened my mouth to speak, to shout, to do anything to prove my own existence, but nothing came out.

Except blood. Gobs and gobs of blood.

My voice had become a ghost, a stolen treasure in this game of supernatural stakes.

I had won the poker game, won the house, but at a cost too horrific to comprehend. The house was not mine; it was its own. I had traded a few cards for my voice, perhaps even for my soul. And as I stood there, voiceless and shivering, the haunting realization washed over me once more: the game was far from over, and I was just another piece on the board.

For the first time, I understood the warnings, the stories, the dread that had filled the eyes of the townsfolk when they spoke of the Dooley Plantation, now Southland. A place from hell with my name on it.

They had been right to fear, right to stay away. And as I was left standing there, in the paralyzing silence, I knew that whatever haunted this place had won this round.

And it was far from done with me.

*****

I woke up in a haze, the events of last night seeming like fragments of a disjointed dream. Had I really heard Roger calling out? Had I really felt that cold grip of dread clutching at my heart? Why had it been impossible to wake up? I'd been trapped in a strange dream. I had been running through tall grass, running for my life. My long dark hair trailing behind me and someone had been calling my name, but not my name.

Keta...come to me!

When I made my way downstairs, I noticed the house was disturbingly quiet—too quiet. Roger was nowhere to be found. My stomach churned with anxiety as I glanced around the empty living room and then, I saw the front door open.

What greeted me left me paralyzed with shock.

Roger was there on the porch, sitting in one of the rocking chairs. But something was horribly wrong. His dark hair had turned an ashen white, as if every pigment had been scared away. His eyes stared ahead, unblinking, seeing but not seeing. His lips moved soundlessly, as if he were trying to speak but couldn't find the words. Dried blood caked the area around his mouth.

What had he done? What was wrong?

I rushed to him, my hands shaking as they touched his face. His skin was cold, so very cold, as if the life had been drained out of him.

"Roger," I whispered, my voice trembling. "What happened to you?"

But he didn't respond. Didn't even seem to recognize I was there. His eyes were lost in some far-away place that I couldn't reach, no matter how much I wished I could.

Fear, more potent and devastating than I had ever felt, enveloped me. As I looked at Roger, at the shell of the man I knew and served, a terrible thought formed in my mind.

Whatever haunted this place had made its first real move, and it had taken Roger as its pawn.

I wrapped a blanket around Roger's stiff body and led him back into the house, his footsteps mechanical, like a puppet on invisible strings. The servants stared in disbelief as we passed them, their eyes filled with a dread that mirrored my own.

"Clara, send for the doctor. Do it now," I commanded her.

We had all sensed that the house was wrong, that something malevolent lurked within its walls. But until this moment, it had been an abstract fear, a ghost story to chill our bones.

Now it was real, horribly real, and we were all prisoners in its tale.

Getting Roger upstairs to his bed proved a challenge but with Sam's help, we achieved it.

As I closed the bedroom door behind us, I couldn't shake the feeling that we were sealing our fates, locking ourselves in with something ancient, dark, and hungry. But the most frightening part was not knowing what it wanted, or how far it would go to get it.

And as I looked once more into Roger's blank eyes, a haunting realization struck me. Roger had not done this to himself. The thing that hated us, that lived here with us had done this.

I propped Roger up on his pillow and tucked the blanket around him. I sat beside him as we waited for the doctor.

The news was not good and Roger became unresponsive. He refused to write, to explain what had happened but I knew he wanted to leave.

And so we did.

We left Southland and we never went back.

Chapter Four—Bruce Southland

I'd always been told I took after my mother more than my father but standing at the threshold of the old plantation house, I couldn't help but feel like I was about to step into my father's shoes.

I'm Bruce Coffee Southland, the only son of Roger Southland, named also after my grandfather on my mother's side. My father had been an imposing man, but he never had my height; I stand at a solid six foot four. My hair was dark like his, though it was a shade closer to black than his once deep brown locks.

At the age of thirty-one, I was in the prime of my life, yet here I was, back in the United States after a career-defining scholarship overseas, summoned by the untimely and downright bizarre death of my father.

I was sure I should feel a certain way about his weird passing, but I hadn't shed a tear since I had not seen him for a decade. After my mother's death, I'd been sent off to school and kept from home. I had long ago given up hating the man for it. I had never lacked for anything, except for perhaps paternal love.

The air was thick with the scent of aged wood and impending rain, a smell I had almost forgotten. Of course, this was not the family home, the Dooley Plantation—now named Southland had been won in a poker game. I'd never been inside the place but was eager to see it along with Emily.

I had every intention of staying away from dear old Dad, diving deep into academia, and distancing myself from a past that felt both surreal and confining. But life had a way of dragging you back to the places you thought you'd left behind.

At least I had not returned alone. I smiled at Emily who walked elegantly beside me.

I had come home to find answers, and perhaps to find a part of my father that had been lost long before his inexplicable death turned him into a local legend.

A few of the townsfolk that wrote to me and spoke of the house as if it were a living being. No one wanted to come out and blame my father for what happened to him, but it was certainly intimated.

My father had been a man of grit and undying willpower, but even he couldn't escape the clutches of whatever darkness had claimed this place.

The front door creaked open, as if inviting me in—or warning me away. I couldn't be sure which. My heart pounded with a mixture of anticipation and dread, echoing the rhythm of footsteps that had come before mine, footsteps that had ultimately led to an unspoken tragedy.

As I crossed the threshold, I felt the atmosphere change around me, thickening like the plot of a story that was far from its conclusion. My father may have lost whatever battle he had been fighting here, but I was determined to turn the page.

Clara had her own crazy ideas, but did I believe her? No, of course not. Why would I believe the woman that had taken my mother's place?

I had followed my father's wishes and granted her a small fortune, but I had insisted she leave town. I'd even seen her off on the coach. It was easy to ignore her tears and pleas.

What I didn't know now was that by entering the Southland plantation, I had just enrolled myself in a game that had been going on for generations, and the stakes were higher than I could have ever imagined.

If I was going to live here with my wife and future children, we needed this place to be respectable. No more talk of curses and ghosts and murder.

I took a moment to stand on the grand porch, its wooden boards groaning as if sighing under the weight of recent history. The mansion stood tall and dignified, a formidable edifice of Georgian architecture. Its facades were adorned with expansive windows, now showing signs of wear, but still remarkably grand. Aged vines climbed the exterior walls, lending an air of timelessness to the place.

The property itself stretched as far as the eye could see. Rolling fields, once full of crops, now lay fallow but still exuded a certain potential. I could visualize them coming back to life, full of color and vitality, if given a little care.

I knew all about horticulture. That had been my field of study and I was quite good at it.

Massive oaks dotted the landscape, their gnarled branches forming intricate patterns against the sky, as if they were trying to tell stories only they knew.

At the far end of the property was a dense forest, its trees standing tall and proud but also forming a barrier, as though guarding secrets best left undisturbed.

There was a lake too, glimmering in the distance, its waters a deep azure that mirrored the sky. It looked so peaceful, a stark contrast to the whispered horrors that supposedly lurked within the depths of the mansion behind me.

Beyond the lake, the land rose into a series of low hills that gave way to a horizon ablaze with the setting sun. Once native American lands or so I'd been told in one of those unwanted letters from nosy neighbors.

For a moment, I was captivated by the sheer beauty of it, beguiled by its promise. This land was rich, fertile—a kingdom waiting for its king, perhaps. I shook my head as I realized I was thinking like my father. Not typical for me.

But the grandeur and potential were marred by an invisible weight, a foreboding sense of dread that seemed to hang in the air. It was as if the land and the house were holding their breath, waiting for something—or someone—to tip the scales.

I glanced at Emily, her wide eyes smiling back at me. Did she sense something? She didn't appear frightened at all. The tales of ghosts and curses had not deterred my young bride.

As I stood there, soaking it all in, I felt a chill creep up my spine. I couldn't escape the feeling that the plantation was scrutinizing me as much as I was scrutinizing it, sizing me up, taking the full measure of my spirit.

Was I a worthy successor to its complex legacy? Only time would tell.

And so, with a deep breath that did little to dispel the unease settling in my gut, I turned back toward the house.

The front door swung shut behind me, and both Emily and I jumped and caught our breath before laughing. I shook my head as I reached for the brass doorknob, its cool metal offering no comfort, and stepped back into the labyrinth of my family's unsettled past.

"Bruce, look at this," Emily whispered as we entered the grand foyer of the house, my eyes were drawn to the intricate patterns on the marble floor, the opulence of a crystal chandelier hanging overhead, and the grand staircase that led to mysteries I could only guess at. "Every time I walk in here I am amazed. This place, it is lovely!"

For a moment, I let myself become wrapped up in the sheer majesty of it all. This was mine. My inheritance. My legacy to either squander or magnify, and hopefully generations of Southlands after me would call this home too. I had legacy on my mind. A solid Southland legacy.

I felt a surge of excitement wash over me, coursing through my veins like an electrical charge. I saw boundless potential before me, lands that could yield bountiful crops, grounds that could be transformed into an Eden of modern living without sacrificing its old-world charm.

This plantation was an unwritten book, and I was armed with a pen full of ink and a mind brimming with ideas.

I knew it wouldn't be easy. I was no dreamer, certainly a realist. Not a gambler like my late father.

And there would be challenges to face, perhaps even confrontations with whatever it was that took my father from this world. I had something that I believed would carry me through. I had centered ambition—a pulsating need to succeed where my father had failed, to turn this house from a whispered horror story into a beacon of prosperity and a testament to the Southland name.

My father, Roger Southland, was a complicated man, but he was not a failure. And I, as his only son, had no intention of letting his legacy be one of defeat. No, maybe I did not love the man, not like a son should love a father but I did love the name. His name. My name.

The shadows that clung to this place, whatever they were, had not counted on dealing with someone like me.

I walked across the room, my steps echoing off the walls, until I reached the fireplace. Above it hung a painting of my father, his stern face as enigmatic as ever. Why had Clara left this here? They'd moved out of Southland only a few months after moving in and that was years ago.

"I've got this, Dad," I whispered, a blend of defiance and promise. "Your story may have ended, but mine is just beginning."

With that, Emily and I unrolled the blueprints I had brought with us—a proposal for the revitalization of the Southland plantation—and spread them out on the grand mahogany table that occupied the center of the room.

It was time to bring this place back to life, to write a new chapter in its storied history. And this chapter would be one of triumph. I would banish any evidence of the wretched Dooley family.

This would be Southland forever.

Just as I was absorbed in the complex details of the blueprints, I felt a gentle touch on my shoulder that pulled me out of my thoughts. Had I lost track of time again? I turned around to find

Emily standing there, a radiant smile gracing her face. Ah, Emily—my anchor in the storm, my lighthouse in the dark waters of uncertainty.

With her fair, golden hair that framed her face like a halo, she looked like something out of a dream. She had this elegance about her, a refined grace that could make a room full of people stop and stare. She was clad in a simple yellow dress that spoke volumes about her understated style.

"Lost in your thoughts again, Bruce?" she asked, her eyes sparkling with a mixture of amusement and affection. "I brought you tea and sandwiches. I don't think you noticed I was gone."

I grinned, folding up the blueprints and setting them aside. "You know me too well, Em. I was just envisioning the future of this place—our future."

Emily walked over and intertwined her fingers with mine. "And it's a future I believe in, as long as we're facing it together."

The room seemed brighter just by her presence, a stark contrast to the shadows and unanswered questions that lingered in other corners of this old home. And it struck me then, more than ever, how crucial she was to my dreams of reviving this place. With Emily by my side, I felt invincible, capable of conquering the very shadows that had consumed my father.

"I love you, Mrs. Southland," I said, pulling her closer and sealing my words with a tender kiss.

"I love you too, Mr. Southland," she whispered back, her words tinged with a love so pure, it could ward off any darkness. "We'll turn this place into something magnificent. It will be the showpiece of the south."

We stood there, hand in hand, facing the grand room that lay before us—its past a complex tapestry of triumph and tragedy, its future a blank canvas waiting for our touch.

In that moment, our united strength shone brighter than any specter that might lurk in the corners of Southland.

And so, with love as my armor and ambition as my sword, I turned back to the table, ready to delve once more into the plans that would shape our destiny. Emily stood by my side, her gaze as steadfast as her love, and I knew that whatever we would face, we would face it together. Eventually she walked over to the nearest window and studied a patch of our property.

She gazed out of the window, her eyes reflecting the hues of the twilight sky. "I've never seen a place so beautiful, Bruce. It's like something out of a dream."

"And it's our dream now, Emily. Our chance to make something beautiful out of a place that has seen its share of darkness."

Emily turned to look at me, her eyes searching mine. "Do you think we'll be able to chase away the shadows, Bruce? To make this place a home?"

I looked into her eyes, radiant even in the fading light, and felt a surge of conviction flood over me. "If anyone can do it, Em, it's us." Emily looked at me, her eyes brimming with a complex tapestry of emotions—anticipation, hope, and a love so potent it could defy even the most malevolent of spirits.

"Home," she echoed softly, as if tasting the word, savoring its promise and its peril.

"Yes, Emily. We're home." The wood beneath our feet felt solid, but I sensed the whispers of the past and the unknown drifting up through the grains. "Let's finish our walk. There's so much to see. These plans can wait."

Taking a deep breath, I slid open the pocket doors. They slid away easily with a solid sound that reverberated through the vast hallway we stepped into. My eyes widened; the inside was a wonder to behold. Polished mahogany and sumptuous rugs met my gaze, a luxurious welcome worn only slightly by the passage of time.

"Good heavens," Emily breathed, her voice tinged with awe as she took in the grand staircase spiraling upwards and the portraits that adorned the walls. The people in those frames seemed to be watching us, their eyes filled with a mix of curiosity and judgment.

"It's even more magnificent than described," I said softly, my voice tinged with a nostalgia that surprised even me.

We ventured further into the large parlor; our footsteps muffled by the thick, decadent carpet. A large fireplace dominated one wall, its mantle graced by a line of antique knick-knacks and a grand mirror that reflected the room in a slightly hazy, golden glow.

"Can you imagine?" Emily said, her voice barely above a whisper, as if afraid to disturb the sanctity of our new home. "Living here, raising a family here, in this grand old place?"

"I can," I replied, pulling her close. "And I plan to do everything in my power to make that dream a reality."

Yet, even as I spoke those words, an odd sensation gripped me. Despite the opulence that surrounded us, there was a heaviness in the air, an almost palpable weight that seemed to say we were not alone, that the house itself was privy to our hopes and dreams—and perhaps had agendas of its own.

"I know it's going to be a lot of work," Emily said, as if sensing my sudden unease. "But we can bring light and life back to this place, Bruce. We can fill it with laughter and love."

I smiled down at her, enchanted by her optimism, willing myself to share it. "Yes, we can, and we will."

As we stood there, marveling at the beauty and grandeur of our new home, it felt as though the very walls were leaning in, listening to our plans, weighing our worth. And for the briefest of moments, I thought I caught a glimmer of something else in the grand mirror above the fireplace—a shadow, a flicker of something darker lurking behind our reflections.

But then Emily laughed, a sweet sound that filled the room, chasing away shadows and doubts, and I told myself it was just a trick of the light.

"We're home," she said, looking up at me. She spun around elegantly, her skirts swirling like flower petals.

"Yes," I agreed, my voice steady, my resolve fortified by her presence. "We're home."

The house seemed to exhale around us, as if settling into this new chapter of its long history. A chapter that we would write together, come what may.

"We should go upstairs and look around, don't you think? I can barely wait much longer and you haven't even touched your tea and sandwiches," Emily complained playfully, her eyes shining with a blend of curiosity and enthusiasm.

"With pleasure," I said, taking her hand as we ascended the grand staircase. The wooden steps creaked under our weight, the sound echoing through the high-ceilinged halls. It was like the house was talking to us, whispering secrets hidden in the woodwork and buried in the walls.

Reaching the top of the staircase, we were greeted by a long hallway, its floor adorned with an ornate carpet that had surely been grand in its time, but now bore the faded elegance of antiquity.

"The master bedroom would be... ah, there it is," I murmured, pushing open the door to reveal a room drowning in both splendor and possibilities. The grand four-poster bed, covered in dusty drapes, stood like a king in exile, presiding over a room of outdated grandeur. The bay windows let in a flood of natural light that seemed to dance on the weathered wallpaper and threadbare rugs.

Emily walked over to the windows and looked out at the sprawling lands that stretched as far as the eye could see. "Could you imagine waking up to this view every morning?"

"Yes, and we will," I said, joining her at the window. "We'll bring this room back to life— restore the wallpaper, replace the drapes, polish the wood until it shines like new."

"I can see it now," she said, her eyes closing briefly as if picturing our future. "A fresh coat of paint, new furnishings, perhaps a chaise lounge right there by the window."

"We'll make it our sanctuary," I vowed, feeling a flush of excitement. But even as I said the words, something tugged at the fringes of my perception.

A fleeting movement in the corner of my eye, like the wisp of a shadow darting across the room. I blinked, looking around, but saw nothing out of the ordinary.

"Yes, we will make it our haven," Emily continued, oblivious to my brief lapse. "Some of the guest rooms should be redone, and perhaps the nursery."

My heart swelled at the idea. "A nursery would be wonderful, a sign of new life in our new home."

As we moved from room to room, each one seemed to tell a story—a narrative of generations past, but also a blank slate, waiting for us to write our own chapter. And yet, there were rooms that sent a chill down my spine; spaces where the air felt denser, colder, as if resentful of our plans to alter its timeworn character.

"Do you feel that?" Emily finally asked as we stepped into what might have been an old study. The room was filled with shelves of books whose titles were obscured by years of dust and neglect. "This room has a chill to it."

"A slight chill," I agreed, trying to keep my voice steady.

She nodded, suddenly serious. "We should have the windows checked, darling. Could be the drafts are coming from loose panes. I wouldn't like to think this place has ghosts." Her words surprised me. Emily wasn't normally one to be superstitious.

I took her hand, gripping it tightly. "It probably is just that. There are no ghosts here, Emily. We'll fix those windows and all will be well."

She smiled, reassured. But as we left the study, I couldn't shake the feeling that something was watching us, evaluating us. I shook my head, dismissing the thought as a trick of an overactive imagination.

The sun dipped below the horizon, casting the sky in shades of pink and orange as Emily and I continued to discuss our plans for each room. The house seemed to grow darker, more contemplative, as if settling into sleep.

"It's getting late," Emily noted, looking out one of the dusty windows. "We should head back to town. It's a long ride."

"Agreed," I said, but as I turned to gather our things, I heard a soft creaking sound coming from the far end of the hall. It was the sound of a door opening slowly, painfully, as if not used for years.

"Did you hear that?" I asked, my eyes meeting Emily's.

"I did," she said softly. "Should we...?"

I nodded. We needed to know. With a newfound apprehension, we moved towards the sound, our footsteps hushed on the aged carpet. The door to the old library was ajar, and as we pushed it open, we found an older man standing in the center of the room. He was dressed in old, worn clothes, his face etched with lines that told a story of hard living.

"Who are you?" I demanded, my heart pounding in my chest.

"I could ask you the same," the man replied, his voice gravelly, but not unkind. "But seeing as you're the spitting image of Roger Southland, I reckon you must be Bruce."

"How do you know my father?" I asked, my hand instinctively reaching for Emily's.

"I worked with him, years ago," the man said. "My name is George. George Wills."

"Why are you here?" I inquired, still uneasy about his unexpected presence. This man was clearly of native American descent, despite his

short haircut and fancy suit. How would my
father know him?

"I had to see you with my own eyes," George
answered, gazing around the room. "I had to
know if the old place had really changed hands.
And to get the measure of you. Do you know
what you're in for here, Mr. Southland? What did
your father tell you about this place? I mean,
before he lost his voice."

"Measure?" Emily spoke for the first time. "What
are you talking about, sir? Who let you in?"

George looked at us, his eyes almost pleading.
"This house isn't meant for you or your young
wife. It's not meant for anyone. No living man
should dwell here. I don't suppose I could buy
this place from you. Buy it and set it ablaze that
is. I will pay you handsomely, young Southland."

"I am in no mood to sell, sir. I think you should
leave our home." My cheeks were burning with
anger. I had a small pistol squirreled away in the
desk. I considered grabbing it.

"You're making a mistake, Mr. Southland. I am
not your enemy. My door is always open to you if

you change your mind. But don't wait until it is too late."

He moved past us, his form almost blending into the increasing darkness. As he reached the front door, he turned back one final time.

"Good luck, sir. If you change your mind anyone in town can point you in the right direction, but don't wait too long." George stepped out into the twilight, leaving us alone in the echoing silence.

"What was that all about? What do we do now?" Emily asked, her eyes searching mine for an answer.

"We stay the course," I said, gripping her hand a little tighter. "Just someone looking to frighten us, Em. That's all. Come on, honey. Let's get back to the hotel."

In the thickening darkness of the impending night, the house seemed to murmur its agreement—or perhaps, its challenge.

Either way, the story of Southland, our story, was far from over.

Chapter Five—Bruce

In the first weeks, it felt as if Southland was embracing us with open arms. It was easy to ignore the stares of the neighbors amidst the excitement of building a new life with Emily.

New plants were brought into the house; fresh paint adorned the walls. But despite these changes, the house seemed to resist us in subtle, disquieting ways.

It started with the little things, odd occurrences that were easy to write off. A door would creak open, untouched, just as I was about to step through. An unexplained draft would extinguish the flame of a candle that had been burning steadily.

More disturbing, the horrible stains on the walls, remnants of Dooley's devilish deeds continued to reappear, no matter how many coats of paint were applied. But that wasn't the worst of it.

The worst of it was the underlying droning of voices, whispers. Two people talking to one another and although the words were indiscernible, the tone sounded menacing.

I got the distinct feeling that these voices were plotting against us. Still, I kept my imaginative thoughts to myself and didn't bring them up to my wife. It didn't matter. She heard the voices too.

"Did you hear that?" Emily would occasionally ask, pulling the blanket closer around her as we sat in the living room. She claimed to hear whispers coming from the hallway, so faint that you could miss them if you weren't listening closely.

"Old houses settle, Em," I reassured her, even as I felt a shiver crawl up my own spine. "They make noises. That's all it is. Could be Jenny talking to herself again. Old people do that sort of thing."

But then came an evening when dismissing these occurrences became impossible.

We were in the dining room, talking about the plans for the south field, when we both heard it—a thumping sound, footsteps coming from upstairs. Heavy, deliberate, and clearly not the product of a 'settling' house. Even I would not believe that. We looked at each other, our eyes locking in a mix of confusion and growing concern.

"You heard it too, didn't you?" Emily's voice was almost a whisper. Jenny hung back in the doorway with a pot of gumbo. The fragrant aroma would have stirred my hunger if not for the fear that welled up within me.

"Yes. Maybe we have a prowler." I admitted. "Maybe it's the inelegant Mr. Wills again. Stay here, you two. I'll go check."

As I ascended the stairs, each step seemed heavier than the last. I told myself I was being irrational, that there was a perfectly reasonable explanation for all of this. Yet, as I reached the landing, an intense feeling of dread washed over me. It was as if I was walking through a thick, invisible mist of unease.

Nervously I cleared my throat as if to give the invader a chance to reveal himself. Perhaps it was that strange fellow George Wills again, come to warn us off the place. I hadn't believed it when I said it but I was grasping at straws now. If he had returned, I'd have to give him a serious tongue lashing.

I found nothing. No intruder, no explanation. But something had shifted in the atmosphere, a change so palpable it was almost like the house itself was warning us.

This is not your place. You have not paid the price.

Fortunately, I heard no voices. No whispers.

Returning downstairs, I looked at Emily, her eyes filled with questions I couldn't answer. "There's nothing there," I told her. Yet even as the words left my lips, I knew that wasn't entirely true. There was a presence in this house, an energy, another resident. Yet whoever or whatever it was, none of us could see but could feel it lurking in the corners, hiding in the walls.

Jenny deposited our meal on the table and then disappeared into the other room shaking her head. Our poor housekeeper seemed quite out of sorts. Fortunately, Emily hired two new maids and they would be appearing for work in a few days. Maybe that would make the old girl happy. Jenny had been with my family since I was young but she had bad mornings. Her ankles and knees hurt her endlessly and she complained about the house constantly.

From that moment on, my own doubts grew louder in my head.

Had we been naive to think we could simply paint over the past? What exactly happened to my father? Could it truly be as Clara said, that something in this house scared him near to death?

Surely there was someone in here. Someone hell bent on wreaking havoc. Playing games. Little did they know I was no game player. I would not tolerate this much longer.

The following morning, I woke up early with the sun just beginning to cast its warm, golden rays over the fields surrounding Southland.

Pulling out the wrinkled maps I spread them over the dining room table yet again as I sipped my stout coffee. Yes, it's true. There was acre upon acre of untapped potential. My eyes traced the boundaries, lingering on patches that would be ideal for cotton, tobacco, and corn.

For the next several days, I threw myself into work. From dawn to dusk, I was out in the fields, marking territories, examining soil quality, and even negotiating with local merchants for seed and equipment. The sun beat down on me, its heat almost unbearable, but I relished it. Each drop of sweat, each moment of exhaustion, felt like a brick laid in the foundation of our new life.

Emily supported me and believed in the dream too. That made all the difference.

But daily life at Southland was marred by the unexplainable. More than once I found my safe standing open yet only I had the combination. Other times, I would find my razor laid open on my pillow, as if someone were threatening me.

I didn't question Emily about any of it. My wife did not have a malicious bone in her body and revealing this discovery to her would only frighten her more. However, if it continued, I would have to confide in her. At least solicit her help in discovering the culprit. Could this be Mr. Wills sneaking into my home to torment me? If he had the ability to crack my safe, why hadn't he taken anything? None of what happened at Southland made any sense.

As I lay in bed one night, my body aching from the physical work I'd been doing, I felt a connection to the land and to my ancestors who had worked it. Yet, George Will's ominous visit came to mind.

What did he mean? Should I pay him a visit?

I glanced over at Emily, peacefully asleep beside me, and then at the old portrait of my father that hung on the wall. It was as if his eyes were fixed on me, filled with both warning and expectation. It was a strange illusion highlighted by the moon casting its pale light through the window, bathing the room in an ethereal glow. There had never been any love in those eyes of his, not towards me, but I had no doubt he'd loved my mother. It was as if when she died, his heart died too.

As sleep began to tug at the corners of my consciousness, I heard it—a soft, almost melodic voice humming, an unfamiliar tune. I opened my eyes and looked toward Emily, wondering if perhaps she was the source. But she lay there, asleep, clearly not the one humming.

The sound seemed to float in from the hallway, faint but clear, coming closer and then drifting away, as though carried by the wind—or by someone, or something, wandering through the hallways of Southland.

With a sense of dread curling inside me, I rose from the bed and tiptoed to the door. As my hand touched the doorknob, the humming stopped abruptly, as if aware of my attention. A shiver ran down my spine. It was a woman's voice.

Could it be old Jenny?

Summoning every ounce of courage, I opened the door. The hallway was empty, veiled in the soft darkness of the night. Yet, as I stood there, peering into the gloom, I saw it—a shadowy figure at the far end of the corridor.

It was but a silhouette, devoid of features, and yet I felt it looking right at me, into me. Then, as suddenly as it appeared, it faded into the darkness, leaving nothing but an icy chill in the air.

I shut the door, my heart pounding, and returned to bed, but not to sleep. Lying there, wide awake next to the woman I loved, I couldn't shake the haunting thought that maybe, just maybe, Southland had its own plans for us— plans that could unfold in terrifying ways I could not yet fathom.

And as the clock ticked its way toward dawn, I knew one thing for certain: we were not alone in this house.

Far from it.

As the minutes stretched into what felt like hours, the room began to grow colder, an unnatural chill seeping through the walls.

My thoughts returned to my father's portrait, and I glanced at it one last time. In that moment, his eyes seemed to change, no longer just filled with expectation and warning but with something darker, more malevolent. His eyes were filled with hatred and his mouth was turned into a twisted grin.

Then, the voice returned, but this time it wasn't just a hum.

It was singing, a haunting lullaby that filled the room, the words indecipherable but filled with a sorrow that was palpable. I felt paralyzed, unable to look away from the portrait as it seemed to come alive, my father's painted eyes staring deeply into my soul.

Just when I thought I couldn't take it anymore, Emily stirred beside me, her eyes opening in a sudden flash. But what I saw in them wasn't the loving gaze of the woman I knew.

It was a hollow emptiness, as if she were momentarily possessed by something—or someone—else.

"He gave me his voice. What will you give me?" she whispered in a voice so unlike her own, echoing the haunting lullaby I had just heard. "What will you give me?"

"Emily?"

Before I could react further, the shadowy figure from the corridor appeared at the foot of our bed, its form more distinct now, but its face still a void. A woman! It appeared like a woman but its face eluded me! Sloping shoulders, petite in size. It reached out, as if to claim something, and in that moment, I felt my voice catch in my throat, I was unable to make a sound.

Emily screamed beside me and the figure vanished, and with it, the chilling voice and the presence in the room. Emily blinked, her eyes returning to normal, and I began to cough. I coughed until I finally found my voice again.

"What was that?" She demanded to know as she clung to me. I didn't know whether to run from her or hold her tight.

As the first rays of dawn broke through the window, I understood the unspoken, chilling truth. The spirits here at Southland didn't want to just scare us off.

It wanted to claim us, piece by piece. And like my father, it wanted to start with my voice—and then maybe it would take my soul.

Chapter Six—Bruce

A few weeks had passed since those first unnerving incidents, and Southland seemed to sink further into an abyss of unexplainable occurrences and tragedy. The plantation was no longer just my home; it was a brooding entity, an amalgam of shadows and whispers that gnawed at the souls of everyone who stepped foot on its soil.

Nobody came to call. Even contractors were hard to find and the blood stains had reappeared, even with the darker paint applied.

Then came the strange deaths.

First, it was Joe, one of the new farmhands. A decent man, diligent and trustworthy. He was harnessing one of the mules—a random shot rang out, they said, although I heard no shot. In some weird twist of fate, Joe was dragged across the plow blade and was sliced nearly in half. He didn't stand a chance.

The news sent ripples of fear among the workers; their faces became masks of dread, their voices hushed. I had never heard of such a freak accident occurring, neither had Emily.

Then, Pete, another hand, simply disappeared and that made no sense at all. Pete had just been promoted and was very excited about his new responsibilities and raise in pay. Some tried to suggest that he'd caught up with a strange woman, but I didn't believe that. Pete hadn't been married to Nancy that long. He seemed genuinely sincere with his affections toward her.

Another one, Thomas Tilbury, simply vanished into the thick woods surrounding the plantation, never to be seen again. The local authorities conducted a perfunctory search, but we all knew they wouldn't find anything. Southland had claimed another soul and then another.

Weeks after a few of the field hands claimed to have seen Thomas peering at them from over a hedge, another reported he chased them, but I didn't know what to make of any of that.

Amidst this whirlpool of despair, a glimmer of hope shone through—Emily was pregnant. Our long hoped for miracle had occurred.

Under different circumstances, this news would have been a cause for celebration, a reason to look forward to the future. Now, it felt like a mixed blessing. How could we bring a child into a home so suffused with unease, so permeated with an unnamable dread?

Emily felt it too, I could see. Her face, usually so radiant, now wore a perpetual look of worry. She stopped walking in the gardens, stopped playing the piano in the evenings. Instead, she took to sitting by the window, staring out into the darkening landscape as if expecting some kind of revelation.

"I see shadows, Bruce. I'm afraid. So afraid," she confessed one early evening, her voice tinged with a vulnerability I had never heard before. "I'm afraid for us, for our baby. This place is cursed; I can feel it in my bones. We should go back. My parents say we are welcome in Virginia. Sell this place to George Wills and be done with it. Please, Bruce!"

I wanted to reassure her, to promise that everything would be alright, but the words stuck in my throat. Because I felt it too—the weight of Southland's malevolent gaze, its insidious whispers weaving through the wind that rustled through the ancient trees.

"This is our land and home, Emily. We must find a way to make this work," I finally managed to say, holding her close. "We have to. For us, for our child. This will be his legacy too." I pretended that I didn't feel her stiffen in my arms.

This wasn't the answer she hoped for. I could hardly believe my own stubbornness.

"Why, Bruce? We aren't poor. We can go anywhere we like." I released her and kissed her forehead. Unable to convince her that she was wrong, I turned back to the work on my desk.

That night, as we lay in our bed, wrapped in a quiet dread, a sudden chill coursed through the room. I could hear the wind whipping around the house, it whistled and almost screamed. Then, a faint sound echoed in the distance—was it crying?

A woman's lament. Not again!

Emily clutched me, so I know she heard it too. We waited in silence, waiting for the door to our bedroom to crack open, but nothing happened. Eventually Emily went back to sleep, but I laid awake the rest of the night listening to the sounds of phantom children giggling and a woman crying.

Could there be any doubt who those spirits might be? Clearly the dead Dooley family remained in the house, but why? Why didn't they seek justice from the man who killed them?

Surely, they would find him burning in hell.

After a week of disquieting events and inexplicable accidents, Old Jenny went missing.

Everyone looked for her, from the kitchen hands to the field workers. Jenny was always the first to be awake and the last to go to bed at night. She was the hardest working soul on the property and although she was generally a woman of few words, everyone respected her.

One morning, Emily and I went to the dining room to find nothing had been attended to. No food prepared, no oven lit. The air was thick with dread.

Emily, pale as a ghost, muttered prayers under her breath, clutching a small cross around her neck. I felt the weight of my own fear, a stone in my stomach, as I went to look for her.

I looked outside first, garnering help from everyone I could find, starting with Sam. The wiry old gardener wrangled all the hands yet our search turned up nothing.

I had no choice but to turn my attention back to the house. I can't say why I looked outside first. Later I would come to understand that it was because I already knew.

I knew she was dead, claimed by the angry spirits of the house.

The search took what seemed to be hours, each minute stretching into an eternity. It was as if the plantation itself was playing tricks on us, obscuring paths, and distorting sounds.

Once I got Emily settled and calmed on the front porch, I decided to climb up to the attic—a place I had avoided all day. In fact, I didn't spend much time in the attic. I never liked the feeling I got up there. The stairs creaked underfoot; each groan a mocking laugh. I was undeterred.

Luckily, it was a bright and sunny day and I could see quite well. And there she was. Old Jenny, seated in an ancient rocking chair that clearly hadn't been touched for years. Her eyes were wide open, staring into a void so dark, it felt like she could see into the very bowels of Hell.

"Jenny?" I asked instinctively. Her face wore an expression not just of terror, but also of recognition—as if she had encountered something, or someone, she had long been expecting. There were no signs of violence, no indications she had been running or hiding. Just a look of final, awful understanding.

As if she'd sat down and given up.

Later, the coroner would say her heart gave out, as if Old Jenny's heart had simply given out from natural causes. But I knew better. Old Jenny's heart had failed, not from age or illness, but from an unspeakable truth so horrifying, it had stopped her very life force.

Southland had claimed her, like it had claimed my father, and as I looked down at Old Jenny, a rush of terrible clarity came over me. We were next.

The discovery of Old Jenny in that forsaken attic was a seismic event that shook the very foundations of Southland—especially Emily. Her face lost whatever color it still had, turning an unsettling shade of white, almost translucent in the dim light.

The staff, usually reserved and unflappable, started whispering prayers like hushed incantations, holding onto crosses, saints' medallions, and other trinkets of faith as if they were lifebuoys in a sea of mounting darkness.

Emily, seeking some form of spiritual refuge, insisted we hold a memorial service for Jenny. So, there we were, assembled in the grand drawing room which felt both too big and too stiflingly small for such an occasion. The air was thick with tension, each glance exchanged heavy with words unsaid, fears unvoiced.

Pastor Williams was a man known for his steadiness and stoic disposition, but even he seemed unnerved. When he stepped forward to speak, his eyes darted around the room in a restless manner, flicking over the faded tapestries and old paintings as if they were malevolent spirits waiting to break free from their frames. His voice wavered as he read from the Bible, and I noticed his hand clutching the good book trembled slightly—a subtle tell, betraying his inner turmoil.

This is ridiculous, I wanted to shout, but I kept my mouth shut.

The sense of unease was palpable, like a living entity among us. The room's antique chandelier flickered as if sympathizing with our collective nervousness, casting erratic shadows that danced ominously on the walls.

It felt as though the very walls and floors of Southland were tightening around us, listening to our murmurs, absorbing our fears.

Everyone felt it. A horrible downshift in the atmosphere of Southland, as if confirming what we had all been too afraid to articulate—that we weren't merely mourners gathered in a room.

We were prey, trapped in a web spun by forces beyond our understanding.

"Lord, we gather here today to remember Jenny," he began, his voice quivering. "May her soul find peace, even if that seemed to elude her in the last moments of her life."

As he spoke, a gust of wind swept through the room, extinguishing the candles on the mantel. A collective gasp filled the room. Pastor Williams cleared his throat and quickly concluded the service. Nobody spoke much afterwards. They just filed out, their eyes averted, as if afraid of catching sight of something unspeakable.

That night, Emily's nightmares began.

She woke up in a cold sweat, her eyes wide with terror, clutching at her belly protectively. "It's the baby," she'd whisper, her voice tinged with an inexplicable dread. "It knows about the baby. It wants the baby."

"And what 'it' are we talking about?" I asked, my voice trembling despite my attempt to sound composed.

"I don't know," she replied. "But it wants something. Something from us, from our family. It's like a debt that needs to be paid."

My thoughts raced back to my father, to the strange circumstances surrounding his silence, his white hair, and the haunting aura that had enveloped him in his last days.

What had he gotten us into? Me and Emily into?

As I lay there, pondering these chilling thoughts, the room seemed to grow colder. The old portrait of my father seemed to watch me, its gaze almost accusatory. I couldn't shake the feeling that Southland's malevolent plans were accelerating, its dark appetite whetted, but far from satisfied.

We had yet to pay the price, and time, it seemed, was running out.

Chapter Seven—Emily Southland

As I stood there, unable to move, the shadowy figures continued their slow march toward me. Their forms were indistinct, but they radiated an aura of menace that was nearly palpable.

I tried to scream, but no sound came out—my voice was trapped in my throat, as stifled as the air around me.

The figures closed in, and just when I thought I could bear it no more, the very earth beneath me seemed to tremble, as though the land itself was rejecting these apparitions.

Just then, the unsettling sky above me ruptured open, and a beam of light shot down, piercing through the darkness. It felt as if some unseen force was battling for the very soul of this place, an ancient struggle beyond human understanding.

I remained frozen in place, my heart pounding in my chest, my breaths short and shallow. As the light fought to disperse the figures, I heard a whisper, like a distant murmur carried by the wind. The words were unintelligible, but their tone was clear—it was a warning.

Leave this place. Leave now...

The shadowy figures recoiled as if pained by the sound, then they slowly dissolved into mist, leaving behind a void even more unsettling than their presence. The light too, retreated, as if acknowledging that its work was done, yet this battle was far from over.

And so I remained standing there, in that uncanny dream-world, trapped between a past yet to be unraveled and a future too grim to contemplate. Southland, or whatever ancient essence lived through it, had secrets it was not yet ready to reveal.

I can't leave. Not without Bruce. I'll make him see sense. I'll convince him that we must leave!

I had no idea who I made this promise too but in that moment, I could feel the turn of the screw. It was then that I felt it—a cold hand grasping my own.

I looked down and saw no one, but the feeling was unmistakable. I was not alone in this forsaken place, and the dread that gripped me was tinged with a sorrow so profound it felt like an abyss. I had the sudden realization that the land was mourning, aching for something—or someone—lost to the folds of time.

In the midst of my dread, shadows began to solidify into more recognizable shapes, becoming almost human, but not quite. They whispered amongst themselves in an unfamiliar, guttural language that echoed hauntingly in the air.

Then, as if commanded, they formed two distinct groups and faced each other. A line was drawn, a threshold none dared to cross. They were preparing for a battle, a shadowy war in a world without time or place.

With my heart pounding like a drum in my chest, I instinctively crouched low behind a gnarled tree that felt both ancient and ephemeral. Whoever clutched my wrist had not manifested but rather abandoned me to watch the shadowy onslaught.

From my hidden vantage point, I watched in both horror and fascination as the two armies clashed, a battle so surreal it defied all logic.

Weapons shimmered in the gloom—blades and spears and unidentifiable instruments of war— all clashing and shimmering in a dance of violence and fury. The sound was an unsettling mixture of cries and whispers, a cacophony that seemed to resonate with the very fibers of my being. I couldn't tear my eyes away, captivated by the unfolding drama, even as every cell in my body screamed for me to run, to wake up, to escape this nightmarish scene.

As the two sides fought, it was as if the very fabric of reality quivered and shook, the land itself serving as a backdrop for a cosmic struggle between forces I couldn't begin to understand. A sense of helplessness washed over me; I was a mere spectator in a conflict that transcended human comprehension.

The air was different now, heavy with an indefinable tension, as if the land itself held its breath, awaiting the next act in a drama that had no end.

As I continued to crouch behind the tree, my mind swirling with questions and fear, I was struck by an awful truth.

Southland was not just a fine home. It was a battleground for something far more ancient, a hidden world just beyond the veil of our understanding. And I, like the generations before me, was now a part of it—whether I liked it or not. Whether I understood it or not.

Still hidden behind the tree, my eyes widened in disbelief as the shadows began to waver, revealing fleeting glimpses of their true forms.

On one side, the features of Native Americans emerged—warriors adorned with feathers and paint, their faces marked with expressions of determination and sorrow.

On the other side were grotesque figures, monsters with gnarled features and twisted forms, nightmarish creatures ripped from the darkest corners of imagination. All were made of shadow, smoke and fire.

The Native American warriors fought valiantly, their ethereal weapons flashing through the air, meeting the monstrous forms with a courage that made my heart ache. It was a struggle that seemed to embody the very essence of Southland, a clash between two worlds—one of tradition and respect for the land, the other of darkness and malice.

But despite their bravery, the Native American warriors began to falter. With each clash, they seemed to lose a bit more substance, their forms becoming more transparent, more insubstantial, as if being erased from existence itself. And finally, as if commanded by some terrible unseen force, they were overwhelmed.

In a heart-wrenching moment, their shadows were forced into the ground, absorbed by the very land they had fought to protect.

The monstrous shadow figures let out a guttural cry of victory, a chilling sound that reverberated through the air and into the depths of my soul.

Sitting there, pressed against the tree, I felt an overwhelming sense of loss and helplessness, as if I had witnessed the turning of a dreadful page in Southland's long and haunted history. The ground beneath me no longer felt like simple earth—it felt like a grave, a final resting place for spirits who had fought and lost.

My eyes filled with tears, not only out of fear but also out of a profound sorrow, a mourning for something invaluable that had been taken, not just from the land, but from all of us who were now bound to it. And as I sat there, enveloped in the night, it became inescapably clear.

Southland was not just haunted. It was a land of lost battles, of ancient conflicts and eternal sorrows. And we, the living, were not merely inhabitants; we were the newest participants in a struggle as old as the land itself.

My heart had barely begun to slow down when a bone-chilling shift occurred.

The monstrous figures seemed to become aware of something new—something that hadn't been there a moment before. I turned my gaze to where they were looking, and there it was: the Southland plantation, standing tall but horribly vulnerable amidst the twilight of this nightmare realm.

Before I could fully comprehend what was happening, the monstrous shadows surged forward like a wave of darkness. They descended upon the plantation with a savagery that defied description.

I could hear screams echoing in the distance—screams of pure, unadulterated terror—as the house lit up in flashes of eerie light. When the shadows retreated, silence fell. A silence far more terrifying than any scream. The Dooley family was no more; they had been brutally, irrevocably claimed by the monstrous entities.

Then, as if sensing my presence, the shadows turned toward me.

Oh yes, they knew all about me!

For a brief, paralyzing moment, our gazes locked—I, a living, breathing human being, and they, unspeakable horrors birthed from the darkest recesses of existence.

The realization hit me like a bolt of lightening--I was next.

My heart pounded in my chest; each beat a drumroll of impending doom. I was still hiding, but it was as if the tree that concealed me had become transparent. The shadows were coming for me; I could feel their malevolent focus narrowing, taste the dread saturating the air.

I couldn't move, couldn't breathe, could only watch as they began their horrifying advance. Every fiber of my being screamed for me to run, to escape this terrible fate, but my body refused to obey. I was trapped in this frozen tableau of terror, unable to avoid what was coming. And they were almost upon me.

With a burst of sheer, primal terror, I screamed—pouring all my fear and horror into that single, piercing note. And, just like that, I was jerked out of the nightmare and back into the waking world.

But the relief I felt was short-lived for they were here. They had followed me.

My eyes snapped open to find one of the monstrous figures from my dream in my room. Its form was hazy but undeniably real, its hands, chillingly cold, were placed on my belly.

I screamed again, this time for Bruce, hoping he'd rush to my side and make this horror go away. But when my frantic gaze landed on the bed beside me, the words died in my throat.

A bone-deep chill spread through me, a feeling colder than the deepest winter. I was in this nightmare alone, a nightmare that had somehow broken free and invaded the waking world—or maybe it was the other way around. And as I screamed for him I realized that my husband was dead and gone. Killed while I dreamed.

Oh, but I knew the horrible truth. Whatever had happened, whatever this entity wanted, it had something to do with the life growing inside me.

My hand instinctively moved to cover my belly, a futile gesture of protection, as the monster's form began to dissolve, retreating into the shadows as if satisfied. And as it disappeared, leaving me alone in a room now filled with unspeakable dread, I realized something far worse than any nightmare. This was not the end.

It was only the beginning.

And then, just when I thought the night couldn't get any worse, she appeared—a ghostly woman materializing in the dim light filtering through the window curtains. It had to be Mrs. Dooley, and the horror of her appearance was amplified by the gruesome gunshot wound dripping from her forehead.

At first, all I heard from her were piercing, unintelligible screams that filled the room like a dissonant symphony of dread. I covered my ears, my own breaths coming out in ragged gasps, my eyes fixed on the terrifying apparition.

Gradually, though, her screams morphed into words, becoming clearer, as if breaking through some kind of ethereal barrier. "They are coming for the baby!" she shrieked, her eyes—oh God, her eyes—filled with a despair that transcended death itself.

The blood in my veins turned to ice. I clutched my belly instinctively, my thoughts racing, fragments of understanding starting to piece themselves together into a horrific tapestry of what had happened—and what was still to come.

And in that moment, terror mingled with a newfound determination. Whatever it took, I would protect my unborn child from the malevolent forces that had claimed so many lives on this accursed land.

Mrs. Dooley's ghostly form began to fade, her message delivered, but her eyes—those haunting, tragic eyes—lingered for a moment longer, as if to underscore the gravity of her warning.

That's when I saw it—the first shadow monster materializing out of the inky darkness. It growled, a guttural sound that sent shivers down my spine, and waved its grotesquely oversized hands. It stomped towards me, each step an echoing thud that reverberated through the very core of my being.

Panic engulfing me, I scrambled around the room, my eyes darting in all directions, desperate for an escape. But as my hand reached for the doorknob, my heart sank—a second shadow monster was blocking my exit, its eyes glowing with a malevolent light.

"Bruce!" I screamed again, but he could not hear me, his lifeless eyes offered no comfort.

I should have left when given the chance. I should have ran!

Somewhere, Mrs. Dooley's spectral voice was screaming, an otherworldly echo that bounced off the walls, adding to my disorientation.

I found myself backed against the window, my hands trembling, my breath shallow. The shadow monster advanced, its grin widening to reveal a void of a mouth so dark, so malevolent, that it seemed like a portal to another, more terrifying world.

The sight of it struck such a chord of primal terror within me that I did the unthinkable—I threw myself out of the window.

As I plummeted, everything went black. Time, space, and consciousness dissolved into a dark abyss, swallowing me whole.

And as I sank into that all-encompassing darkness, the last thought that raced through my mind was that this was only the beginning of sorrows.

Chapter Eight—Aracely Bulkhalter

It was my dream come true. Southland Plantation, sprawled before me like an old treasure begging to be polished and shown off to the world. Why it felt so familiar to me, I could not say.

As I walked along the creaking wooden boards of the grand old mansion, my mind buzzed with ideas—each room had its own vibe. This place would be the best wedding venue anyone had ever seen. It made absolutely no sense to have such a dream come true. If not for the tragic loss of my father, this would not have been possible.

Southland was old, but she had good bones, I told myself. Still, these bones would require a lot of money to get her ready for showtime.

I was aware of the stories about the old house, of course.

For the past decade, Southland had been a haunted house attraction—thrilling teenagers and terrifying fear seekers. Before that, it was sold repeatedly like a hot potato; former owners couldn't bear to keep it for long. Naturally that fueled the mythos of Southland, but I wasn't one to be frightened off by a few stories.

Honestly, I had always been fond of spirits, the ghostly kind I mean, but it wasn't like I was some kind of ghost whisperer. Not the drinking kind—that was my mother's spirit of choice. I figured the stories would add a dash of authenticity to the place, maybe even give it a charming, historical aura, but the ghost stories didn't really factor into the equation.

I had money to invest and owning a wedding venue had been my dream for as long as I could remember. Mind you, I never imagined my own wedding. But I loved the idea of helping others make their day perfect.

Yet, as I walked through Southland with the deed in my possession, the air buzzed with a strange energy. It was almost as if the very walls and floors, steeped in a tea of bygone lives, wanted to spill their secrets.

As I ventured further into the house, I couldn't ignore the disrepair. How had I walked through here before completely ignoring what I, the new owner, would be facing.

Still, the grand staircase even with its chipped wood and peeling paint, managed to project an aura of old-world grandeur. Cobwebs hung like tattered lace curtains, some real, some Halloween decorations gave the place a macabre air. Dust covered the once-gleaming marble floor, evidence of further neglect. The high ceilings were stained and discolored; their former glory now hidden beneath years of water damage.

And then there were the portraits—faded oils of faces whose names I didn't know. *Who would leave these behind?* The portraits lined the walls in gilded frames that had seen better days, their eyes following me as I moved, as if they were assessing me.

Amidst the general decline were remnants of its most recent incarnation as a haunted house attraction. Spooky dolls with missing eyes and unraveled yarn hair sat in corners, their faces twisted into permanent grimaces.

Mannequins dressed as ghouls and witches stood haphazardly, some leaning against walls as if they, too, had given up on maintaining their posture. Strobe lights, disused fog machines, and rubber bats littered the floor—cheap thrills that seemed almost insulting to a place that had its own authentic narrative of haunting.

Well, Aracely, you sure have a ton of work to do. Too bad you don't have a crew of friends to help you make this the showplace of your dreams.

But despite all this—or perhaps because of it—I felt an overwhelming sense of potential. I was weird like that. Always ready to accept a challenge.

I felt a shiver run down my spine, a cocktail of trepidation and exhilaration. *Ghosts or no ghosts, this place was going to be magnificent. And the spirits? Well, they'd just have to get used to me.*

Funny enough, my first encounter with the spirits of Southland had been during its stint as a haunted house venue.

I was walking through the grand ballroom, filled with those same fake cobwebs and mannequins, when I felt it—a cold breeze, unlike the staged spookiness around me. It was as if someone had walked right through me. Not scary, just...intriguing.

In that moment, I knew.

I knew I'd be the one to buy this place and bring it back to life—figuratively speaking, of course. I had this inheritance money sitting in a bank account, gathering dust for over a year. It was time to do something with it, something big. So, I did it.

I bought Southland Plantation, lock, stock, and barrel.

As I stood in the now-empty ballroom, absent of some of the Halloween gimmicks, but brimming with authentic eerie charm, I felt the same chill again. It passed through me, leaving me more invigorated than frightened. It was as if the house itself was welcoming me, acknowledging my plans.

"I won't let you down," I whispered to the room, to the air, to the spirits that I was certain were listening. I was going to keep my promise, no matter what—or who—stood in my way.

I decided it would be a good idea to cleanse the property with sage. *That's what people did to ward off spirits, right?* I came from a home that believed in using the stuff. I burned sage in every room, walking through the grand corridors with the stick burning in an abalone shell. The thick, herbal smoke spiraling in the air.

Next on the agenda was getting a shaman out here to bless the property, maybe sprinkle some blessed herbs around. My cousin, Susan recommended a young man, Ryan was his name, but he preferred to go by Red Sky. He sounded professional and was happy to come out to perform a cleansing ritual on the property. I was quite proud of myself to have at least a few tasks done.

After the phone call, I stood in the middle of the foyer, suddenly feeling the gravity of my decision to buy this place. But I was not afraid, and I wanted the spirits—Southland itself—to know that.

I grabbed an empty cardboard box from the stack I had brought with me. Time to get my hands dirty.

Methodically, I began picking up discarded trinkets, broken toys, and shreds of costumes that had been left behind over the years. The dolls with their sinister smiles, the rubber snakes and spiders, the disheveled mannequins—they all went into boxes.

The amount of clutter was overwhelming, but that didn't deter me. I had always been the kind of person who thrived on transforming chaos into order, mess into potential.

That was a lesson I learned early on. Between my parents, one a traveling truck driver and the other a consistent drunk, I was accustomed to depending on myself to make my world a happy, somewhat orderly place.

The back of my pickup truck was ready and waiting, eager to be filled with what was essentially the haunted debris of Southland. I planned to haul all this junk off to the scrapyard later.
Out with the old, to make room for the new.

Besides, there was something cathartic about physically removing the junk, as if each piece I picked up brought the estate closer to the magnificent wedding venue it was destined to become.

As I sweated and moved from room to room, I was struck by how the house seemed to be cooperating. Maybe it was just my imagination running wild, but I felt like the atmosphere had shifted ever so slightly, as if the very walls were sighing in relief.

No. It hadn't enjoyed being a Halloween attraction at all.

With each box I filled, I could almost hear the property urging me on, like a faded starlet desperate for a return to the limelight.

As I paused to take a breather, my eyes caught a glimpse of an old photograph hanging lopsided on the wall. It was a sepia-toned image of a family, presumably one of Southland's previous owners. Their faces were stern, perhaps even unhappy. It made me think of my own roots— Native American on my mother's side. My ancestors were no strangers to lands infused with spirits and legacies. Maybe that's why I felt so connected to this place, felt an innate understanding of its complexities.

Just as I was pondering this, my phone buzzed on the wooden table where I'd left it. It was Mom. "Aracely, come home now," she demanded, skipping any pleasantries. "This isn't a game. Don't mess with things you don't understand."

"For heaven's sake, Mom, it's just a house," I retorted, but my voice betrayed a hint of doubt. "An old, rundown house that I'm going to turn into something beautiful."

"You're walking on ancient grounds, my girl," she warned. "You should know better. I had a dream. A warning. It was a real dream!"

As much as I wanted to brush off her concerns, a tiny knot of apprehension formed in my stomach. I looked around at the decaying opulence, the eerie keepsakes, and the restless shadows stretching across the walls as the sun dipped below the horizon. For the first time, I felt a sliver of doubt creep in.

I snapped back to reality. "I've got to go, Mom. Stop worrying. The shaman will come and cleanse the property in a few days."

"A shaman?" She paused, mulling it over. "Well, if you won't listen to me, maybe you'll listen to him. Just be careful, Aracely. Some spirits aren't to be trifled with."

With that ominous warning echoing in my ears, I hung up the phone. Despite my initial bravado, I had to admit that Mom's words struck a chord. Was I being too cavalier about the energies enveloping Southland? Was my ambition clouding my judgment?

Shaking off these thoughts, I resumed my work, but I couldn't completely shake the feeling that Southland wasn't just challenging me—it was warning me.

No sooner had I put down the phone than it buzzed again. It was Mom, once more. She did this sometimes. Got so drunk she forgot we'd just talked. Or she'd remember something else she wanted to say. I sighed and answered, "What is it now?"

"You're messing with darkness, Aracely," she slurred. Yes, the haze of alcohol in her voice was unmistakable. "The dancers were there. They danced until they were dead!" She bombarded me in her native language, but I couldn't ignore the fear in her voice.

"Mom, stop it. We'll talk later," I said, my voice tinged with exasperation and disappointment. "When you're not drunk."

Ignoring my words, she launched into another string of Cherokee phrases. One I knew quite well. She basically called me an ignorant half breed. She'd been saying that for years and the pain never got any easier. At least hearing it didn't make me cry anymore. Her tone was urgent, desperate even. My grasp of the language was shaky at best, but the gravity in her voice was unmistakable.

"I can't do this with you right now, Mom," I said, frustrated, and hung up the phone. But despite my irritation, her words lingered in my mind. Her insults and her warning. Yes, it was a warning, one that resonated within the very core of my being.

For a moment, I stood still, surrounded by the relics of Southland's murky past.

Was my mother's intoxicated rambling merely the product of too many drinks, or was it a genuine cry of concern rooted in a wisdom I had yet to understand? My hand rested on an old, tattered doll as I pondered this, its glass eyes almost pleading with me.

The weight of generations, both mine and Southland's, seemed to press on me from all sides.

I shook my head. "Get it together, Aracely," I muttered to myself. "You've got work to do." Yet, as I grabbed another dusty box and picked up more trash, I couldn't quite dismiss the haunting Cherokee warning my mother had uttered.

It was as if the house and the land itself were listening, waiting to see what I'd do next.

"Kawihiyanvi tsiyuhi tla nv Aracely! Ihiya Nunnehi!" My mother's words echoed through my heart and mind.

"You will dance until you're dead too, Aracely! Beware the Nunnehi!"

Chapter Nine–Aracely

I dragged a cot into the corner of the parlor, my eyes scanning the dilapidated room with a blend of exhaustion and ambition. The upstairs bedrooms were no-go zones for now—filled with peeling wallpaper and decades-old grime. No way was I camping out up there tonight. The parlor would have to do.

At least I had hot water so I indulged in a hot shower. Strangely enough, the bathroom was the cleanest room in the house. I towel dried my hair and changed my clothes before heading back downstairs for some sleep. Even though I was dead tired, I wasn't quite sleepy yet.

Opening my laptop, I sifted through my inbox, shooting off replies to florists, caterers, and all sorts of vendors who were interested in working with me once Southland was up and running as a wedding venue. That would be at least six months out but it felt so good to get the ball rolling, to get one step closer to transforming this place.

The arches I'd ordered for the outdoor chapel were set to be delivered soon. I probably jumped the gun on that since the yard wouldn't be ready for venue usage until next spring. Still, it felt good to have found and secured them. People loved outdoor weddings and there were so many lovely oak trees out here.

And then, right as I was in the middle of a sentence about fabric swatches, it happened.

The air grew colder. The dim light from my laptop screen cast eerie shadows on the walls, and for a moment, it felt like the room held its breath. *Was I getting a chill?* I grabbed the towel beside me and attempted to dry my hair a bit more.

I shook off the sensation, attributing it to the late hour and my tired mind. But as I was about to return to my emails, a sudden flicker of light caught my attention. It was as if the room itself blinked, and for a brief second, the walls seemed to ripple and distort, like a mirage.

Holy heck! I sat up straighter, my heart pounding. *Was this some sort of paranormal activity, or just my mind playing tricks on me?*

My cursor hovered over the "Send" button. But just then, a gust of wind blew through the room, moving the dinghy curtains that hung over the large parlor windows. The hallway light flickered off and I was plunged into darkness, the light from my laptop screen now harsh and glaring.

I closed the lid, my eyes darting around the room. Get it together, Aracely. The walls are just walls, the shadows mere absences of light. And yet, there was a weight to the darkness, a palpable sense that I wasn't alone. It was hard to describe or even understand.

Suddenly afraid of the shifting darkness, I scrambled for my phone, eager to switch on its flashlight, when I heard a discernable noise. Yes, it was a faint whisper, a voice as if carried by the invisible wind itself, swirling around the room before vanishing into the ether.

I couldn't make out the words, but the message was clear: something was stirring, and whether I liked it or not, Southland was waking up. To my horror, the whispering didn't stop.

I felt my heartbeat synchronize with each haunting syllable, thumping louder and faster. My eyes shot toward the dusty curtains that framed the parlor windows. They shifted again and rustled as if dancing to an invisible wind.

"Okay, Aracely, keep your head," I mumbled to myself, summoning the courage to investigate this strange activity. I took a deep breath and stood up, my phone's flashlight illuminating the room like a lone star in the night sky.

I stepped closer to the window. I knew it was closed. What could be causing that movement? My shaking fingers reached for the fabric. Just as I was about to pull back the curtain, a sharp knock echoed from the front door, freezing me in my tracks. My heart leapt to my throat—I nearly screamed.

When I finally caught my breath, I stepped back and away from the window. "Who in the world could that be?" I mumbled to myself.

Carefully, cautiously, I navigated my way through the dark hallway towards the front door, each step accompanied by a chorus of old floorboards groaning under my weight.

As I walked, the hall light came back on with a loud snap.

After what felt like an eternity, I arrived at the door. Taking another deep breath, I opened the door, half-expecting to come face-to-face with some terrifying specter. To my immense relief, it was Susan, my cousin, standing there with a bright smile and a box of snacks under one arm, and a bottle of champagne in the other.

"Susan! What are you doing here?" I gasped, still catching my breath.

"I heard you were taking on the biggest project of your life, and I thought, 'What better way to celebrate than with some champagne and good company? The good company being me, of course." She walked in, filling the gloomy interior with her bubbly energy.

"Wow, thank you! You have no idea how much I needed this," I said, as we hugged tightly.

As Susan set down the snacks and uncorked the bottle, the lingering fear that had consumed me started to fade, like mist under the morning sun. She was my touch of normalcy in a world that seemed to be spiraling into the inexplicable.

But as we toasted to new beginnings, I couldn't shake the thought that Southland wasn't done revealing its secrets. And whether those secrets would make or break my dreams remained to be seen.

Susan settled onto a cushion next to my makeshift cot, her eyes scanning the parlor. "You've definitely taken on a lot, Cuz. But if anyone can turn this place around, it's you." I smiled at her, grateful for the vote of confidence. But as I looked back, I noticed she was shivering, her arms wrapped around herself.

"Are you okay? Is it too cold in here?" I asked. *Was she feeling the weirdness too?*

"A little, maybe." Susan glanced around the parlor; her eyes wide. "You know I don't believe in spooky stuff, but there's something... unsettling about this place," Susan admitted. "I know you don't want to hear that but..."

I sighed. "You're telling me. Wait a second, Susan. Did Mom send you here to check on me?"

"Give me a break. No, of course not. We're not on speaking terms, again," Susan replied, rolling her eyes. "But let's be real, she needs rehab. I love Auntie Rae, but she's a bit nuts."

"I know," I said softly. We both knew it but saying it out loud made it painfully real.

Susan looked around the room again, her eyes lingering on the dark corners. "Look, why don't you come spend the night with us? The couch is pretty comfy and Jarod would love to see you."

The mention of Jarod made me hesitate. I didn't particularly like him, especially after he made a few inappropriate passes at me. But the look in Susan's eyes—part concern, part genuine affection—made it difficult to refuse. Not to mention, the longer we sat here the more spooked I got. Maybe I should have held on to that tiny apartment of mine a little longer.

"Alright, you win," I said, giving in. "Let me just pack up a few things."

As I grabbed my bag and laptop, something deep within me breathed a sigh of relief. I was grateful to escape, if just for one night, from the overwhelming presence of Southland and its haunting whispers.

As I closed the door behind me, I couldn't help but wonder what I was running from. And even more worrisome, what would be waiting for me when I returned.

As I turned the key in the ignition of my truck, the engine growled to life, breaking the thick silence of the Southland estate. I followed Susan's car, its taillights glowing like the eyes of some nocturnal creature as we made our way down the long, winding driveway. The towering trees seemed to lean in, their branches like arms yearning to pull me back.

That's when I heard it—the drumming.

A rhythmic pulse, deeply resonant and unmistakably Native American, filled the air. It was as if the earth itself had opened its mouth to speak in beats and booms. I slowed down, letting Susan's car pull ahead and turn onto the highway, now a distant glow of red.

I searched the vast front lawn, trying to locate the source of the sound. My gaze landed on an ancient tree, gnarled and imposing, that seemed to stand as a sentinel at the edge of the property.

My radio was off, my phone was silent; the drumming was real, but where was it coming from?

For a fleeting moment, my vision shifted, and I saw them—translucent figures circling the tree, their feet barely touching the ground, their faces set in expressions of fierce determination. They were dancers, Cherokee by the look of them, moving in haunting synchrony, their bodies shimmering as though woven from the mists of time itself.

And then they were gone, evaporating into the heavy air, leaving only the echo of their drumming in my ears. I was both awed and unsettled, my hands gripping the steering wheel as if it were a lifeline.

With a deep breath, I shook off the vision and thrust the truck back into drive. The wheels skidded momentarily on the gravel before catching, and I sped out of the driveway as if chased by the very spirits I had just witnessed.

As I joined Susan on the highway, my mind raced. The haunting energy of Southland was waking up, making itself known in ways both wondrous and terrifying. What had I gotten myself into? And what would it take to transform this haunted land into the vision of beauty and celebration that I had seen in my dreams?

As I drove on, the drumming slowly faded away, swallowed by the wind rushing past my window.

But the questions remained, settling in the pit of my stomach like stones, heavy with the weight of histories—both known and yet to be discovered.

When I walked into Susan and Jarod's cramped trailer, the air felt heavy, weighed down by the scent of stale cigarettes and damp upholstery. *Comfy couch, my behind.* Still I smiled and thanked my cousin for the invite. The space was a hodge podge of mismatched furniture and piled-up dishes, a stark contrast to the grandeur, albeit decayed, of Southland.

After an awkward embrace from Jarod, one that lingered a few seconds too long for my comfort, the three of us sat down in the living room, the tattered cushions of the sofa sagging beneath us.

We cracked open some beers, filling the silence with sips and small talk. Jarod's grin seemed to stretch wider with each bottle he emptied, but his eyes never met mine. *Thank God above.*

I couldn't help but wonder what Susan saw in him. She was vibrant and strong-willed, a woman who deserved a partner who appreciated her, not someone who reduced her life to the boundaries of this rundown trailer.

In high school, Susan was the girl voted most likely to succeed. She was beautiful with her vibrant brown eyes, shiny black hair and athletic build. Then Jarod came along, like some sort of energy vampire and sucked the life right out of her. I made it clear at the beginning of their relationship that I didn't trust him—or like him and that caused a rift between Susan and I for a bit.

In the end, I decided losing my friendship with my one and only cousin wasn't worth it. I tolerated the jerk for her sake—as long as he didn't push me too far.

Finally, Susan brought me a pillow and some blankets, their colors faded and fabric worn. "Here you go. Do you need anything else?"

"Nope. I'm good. Might brush my teeth, but I'm exhausted. It's been a long day."

I thanked her with a hug but already regretted my decision to come here. Still, I was grateful for the temporary respite from Southland's restless spirits, or whatever was going on at my property.

Later in the night, I heard footsteps padding softly toward the kitchen.

It was Jarod, his figure looming in the dim light as he stopped by the couch where I lay. "Can't sleep?" he asked, his silky voice carrying a note of smugness. I barely looked at him, murmuring that I was tired and didn't feel like talking. I turned my back to him and pretended to go back to sleep. I couldn't see him, but I imagined his grin remained unbroken.

Confident, inappropriate jerk. A few seconds later, he sauntered back to the bedroom.

Sleep was a series of tossing and turning, my thoughts punctuated by the occasional creak of the trailer's walls. When dawn finally broke, its light barely trickling through the worn-out curtains, I felt as though I had been wrestling with my own restless soul.

I got up, careful not to wake Susan or Jarod, folded the blankets, and stacked the pillow neatly on the couch. With a sigh, I stepped out of the trailer, leaving behind its confining walls and the stifling atmosphere.

I would text her a thank you in a bit, but there was no sense in waking Susan up this early.

As I drove back to Southland, my thoughts remained on Susan. She deserved more than this, more than a life confined to the boundaries of a trailer with a man who didn't appreciate her. *Well, all I can do is be there for her when the mess hits the fan.* And as for me, despite the challenges that awaited at Southland, I knew that I had a mission—to transform it into something magnificent, come what may.

I had ghosts to face, both literal and metaphorical, but at least they were in a place that promised potential and grandeur, not in the suffocating stillness of a rundown trailer. Not that I was judging her, but I knew she could do so much better than to saddle herself with Jarod.

The aroma of freshly brewed coffee and sizzling bacon welcomed me as I pushed through the door of Mae's Diner, a local fixture I'd frequented since childhood. Mae, the owner, greeted me with her usual warmth, though her eyes looked more puzzled than pleased to see me. Over the years, Mae appeared to shrink, getting skinnier and shorter. Or maybe it was just that I was so much older than when I first met her.

Once upon a time, she and my mother had been friends. Thankfully she never asked about her anymore.

"Aracely, long time no see, hon. Ready for some coffee? Hey, I heard you bought Southland," she said, pouring coffee into a chipped mug. Her voice wasn't so much inquisitive as it was tinged with concern.

"That's right," I replied, eager to move past the subject. "Can I get a biscuit with that coffee?"

"Sure can. I've got some hot ones, just came out of the oven. Be right back. You want bacon or sausage?"

"Neither. Just the biscuit and some jelly, please."

While waiting for my order, I chatted with some of the other patrons, folks I'd grown up around, but hardly spoke to these days. As the conversations veered towards my new venture, skepticism laced their words.

Bob, an odd old man who'd seen more than his share of town history, leaned over the counter. "There's no shortage of stories about that old place. My grandfather lived there for about two weeks back in the fifties. Couldn't take the feel of the place. Can't say I've ever been there though. Hey, you aren't offering tours, are you?"

I was intrigued by his revelation, but not sure I really wanted to get the details. I guess it didn't matter. "No, sir." Bob kept talking as he scooted to a bar stool closer to me.

"Did you know the nunnehi were said to roam those lands?" he questioned, his eyes narrowing. "It's true. We all know about it. Even the white settlers knew about them. Pure evil they are."

The word sent a chill down my spine, echoing my mother's slurred warning: "Beware the nunnehi!"

Bob seemed to relish the unease that flashed across my face. "They're shadow spirits, Aracely. Legends say they occupied that land long before any of us. And they don't take kindly to trespassers. If you stay there, they'll want their payment."

"I'm not a trespasser. There will be no additional payment. I already paid a small fortune for the house and property. It's my land now," I retorted, annoyance creeping into my voice. Bob shrugged, a look of "don't say I didn't warn you" crossing his weathered face. I noticed the rest of the coffee shop went eerily quiet.

Grabbing my coffee and biscuit, I tossed a few bills onto the counter. "Thanks for the history lesson, but I've got work to do," I said curtly, more to myself than to anyone else.

As I walked out of the diner, my shoes slapped against the worn linoleum, each step fueling my determination. Skeptics be damned. Legends or no legends, Southland was my project, my vision. And come hell or high water—or even nunnehi—I was going to make it work.

I turned off the main road and onto the gravel driveway leading to Southland, I felt the ambience shift—thickening, almost stifling.

A strange fog encased the property, swirling in ghostly tendrils around the skeletal trees and dilapidated fencing. The road itself was oddly clear, as though the mist refused to cross its boundaries.

And then there was the silence—an unnatural stillness that seemed to absorb all sound, filling the air with an unsettling void. No chirping of birds, no rustling of leaves; just an eerie, tomb-like hush that seemed to drape over everything like a shroud.

Yes, it was as if I'd stepped into an open grave...

My heart pounded in my chest as I parked and approached the front door, which swung ajar in an almost welcoming fashion.

"Hello?" I pushed it open fully and stepped inside, only to gasp at what I saw. There were footprints. Everywhere. And I do mean everywhere.

But not just any footprints—these were moccasin prints, smudging the faded wallpaper and scarring the creaky wooden floors. And they weren't confined to just the ground. They climbed the walls, veering onto the ceiling in a defy-all-logic sort of way, as though gravity had taken a holiday. The creepy sight made me want to barf.

My eyes darted around, half-expecting to see some phantom figure responsible for this chaos. But there was nothing—only that consuming silence, now pulsating with an almost malevolent energy.

Panic clawed at my insides. I fumbled for my phone and dialed Red Sky's number. My voice trembled as I spoke. "Can we move our appointment up? Something's happening at Southland. Something...I can't explain. I need your help."

There was a brief pause on the other end, long enough to make me wonder if the void had swallowed my words too. Then, Red Sky's deep voice cut through the stillness, a lone anchor in this sea of inexplicability.

"I'll be there," he said. And for the first time since buying this place, I felt a sliver of relief— intermingled with a dread I couldn't shake.

I felt an uncontrollable need to document this inexplicable event. Trembling hands or not, I navigated to the camera app and began taking pictures. The moccasin prints looked even more unsettling through the lens, somehow magnified in their impossibility.

How was this possible? Was this some sort of prank?

For a moment I wondered if perhaps Bob and his cohorts had something to do with this, but there was no way. Maybe my mother wanted to scare me back home? Or it was Jarod? No. No way. The pattern of the prints was impossible. You'd need a twelve-foot extension ladder to reach the ceiling.

I moved through each room, capturing the prints as they scaled walls and traced haunting paths across ceilings. The camera clicked and with each shot, I felt a mix of disbelief and a deepening sense of urgency.

For whatever reason, having those photos in my phone felt like holding onto a piece of tangible evidence in a world that had suddenly turned surreal.

And as that fog outside swirled in intricate patterns, I clung to the notion that, with Red Sky's help, I might be able to unravel the mysteries that Southland seemed so eager to stir back to life.

Still, I couldn't stay inside the house. Not in this now freezing, unyielding mansion. I stepped out onto the porch and settled into a creaky rocking chair, shivering both from the chill and the thought of the ghostly footprints I'd just documented.

It had been a long time since I had a smoke, and the urge was almost overwhelming. But instead of making the trek to the not-so-convenient store five miles away, I sat there, watching the fog as it twisted and coiled around the ancient trees on the property, as if the land itself was holding its breath.

I felt a mixture of dread and expectation, my heartbeat syncing with the far-off rhythm of a drum that might have existed only in my imagination.

But it wouldn't cease and the reservation was too far away to hear such drums.

What I was hearing had to be from the other side.

But the other side of what?

Chapter Ten—Red Sky

As I drove along the winding road to Southland, the property Aracely had bought, my mind sifted through the research I'd done on her place. More specifically, the land. It was a patchwork quilt of history and folklore, each square sewn with threads of conflict and mysterious happenings.

Before the string of bizarre murders that targeted the white families, the area had been soaked in the blood of many Cherokee people.

Legends were whispered through the tribe, passed down to each generation from the elders to the young. Stories they were, warning the vulnerable about the nunnehi. As a student of anthropology, I knew this to be a common practice in many cultures.

"Stay away from the creek, or the swanshi will drown you."

"Don't go up the mountain alone, or the ttavini will devour you!"

The ancient warnings were acceptable ways to warn children from staying away from the deep waters of the river, and to avoid climbing the higher ground and falling or encountering a cougar. But plain warnings were not enough to capture the imagination—and fear of the children.

But the nunnehi were different.

The shadowy spirits were said to dwell on the land long before the Cherokee or the whites. They came from somewhere dark and dangerous, but no one knew where.

The stories told today were of ethereal figures, darting between trees in the moonlight, only visible from the corner of one's eye, their whispers a chilling melody in the wind.

According to oral tradition, they were called the People of Fire and Smoke, unlike the Cherokee who were of Earth and Water.

To make the myth even more terrifying, the elders still say that a whole village of Cherokee warriors had supposedly vanished into the mists of history after marching into the forest to confront these enigmatic entities. They were holy men, sacred dancers who had the power to subdue the People of Fire and Smoke.

Or so they believed.

The closer I got to Southland, I noticed a strange fog along the roadside. It was strange because it was broad daylight and this hilly area wasn't known for collecting fog. The closer I got to Aracely's home, the thicker the fog seemed to become.

It hung heavy over the treetops, drifting and curling like tendrils of smoke from an evil pipe. It was as if the land itself was exhaling its years of suffering and secrets.

And here I was, entering this charged atmosphere, armed with a blend of skepticism and faith, trying to peel back layers of a history that might be better left undisturbed.

I couldn't shake the feeling that I was about to plunge into an ocean of untold and submerged sorrows. But whether it would lead to clarity, or drag us all deeper into a hellish enigma, only time—and Southland—would tell.

I couldn't help but think of Susan, Aracely's cousin, as I got closer to my destination.

Susan and I had been friends for years, ever since we met at a community event. She was lively, outspoken, and beautiful, a combination that lit up any room she walked into. I was pretty sure I had seen Aracely before, but we had never formally met.

I had carried a secret crush on Susan for what felt like forever, but eventually I came to terms with the fact that our paths were diverging. She married Jarod, and well, I never sensed that she saw me as more than a friend. She did as much as tell me so one sad afternoon.

I didn't need her to tell me twice.

I tucked those feelings neatly into the rearview mirror of my mind and focused on the road ahead. I shook my head determined to be mindful of Aracely Burkhalter's dilemma. I absently wondered how alike Aracely and Susan might be.

Why would someone like Aracely, from a mixed heritage and a complicated relationship with her roots, buy a place like Southland? I knew that much about her. What was Aracely hoping to find, or perhaps, escape? There must be a story there.

No, Southland was no ordinary patch of earth; it held mysteries that the elders spoke of with hushed voices. These mysteries went far beyond the reservation. The entire town knew about Southland. Some treated it as a paranormal joke, others avoided it at all costs.

Who in their right mind would want to make that old house a wedding venue? Did the girl truly know what she was getting into?

These were questions my grandfather asked. Aloud of course. I had no answers, but it didn't dissuade me from coming here.

The air was thick with an energy that was hard to define. It was as if the spirits of the land were watching, waiting to see what I would do next.

As I drove, more of my grandfather's words echoed in my mind.

Last night, we'd sat together, poring over old texts and I listened to stories about the enigmatic land that Aracely now owned. I knew much about the legendary nunnehi, I mean I'd graduated with high honors. I hadn't exactly done much with my master's degree, but I still held the knowledge.

"Some battles are better left unfought," Grandfather warned, his eyes meeting mine with an intensity that brooked no argument. I offered none. "Whether you believe in the nunnehi or not, something—or someone—has been causing these tragedies for generations, maybe even longer. It is a cursed place," he added, his voice tinged with a gravity I rarely heard.

Grandfather went on to share the oral tradition with me; all about the sacred dancers, the holy men who had once set foot on this land, hoping to cleanse it of whatever dark forces lurked there. They had been revered spiritual leaders, and yet they had vanished without a trace.

The implication was clear: if even those powerful individuals couldn't face whatever haunted Southland, what chance did the rest of us have?

Especially me. An unbelieving shaman. A shaman in name only.

I had inherited Grandfather Jack's mantle, but I couldn't lie to myself. Was I qualified to be a man of faith and power?

"The girl should leave," Grandfather Jack concluded. I was taken aback by his words. He rarely ever spoke in such stark terms. The warning gripped me.

Could I really help Aracely? Should I even try?

My car's headlights barely pierced the thick fog, I couldn't shake my grandfather's stern warnings. Each turn of the wheels seemed to echo his words. "Some battles are better left unfought, grandson."

I passed the faded sign indicating that Southland was only a few more miles away, and my stomach churned with a mix of anticipation and dread. I thought about the sacred dancers who had vanished, as if swallowed by the earth itself.

Fear overwhelmed me. A strange, sudden fear and I was never afraid. I was, at heart, a man of science. I suddenly came to a stop. My foot pressed the brake pedal; I was torn between turning back or pressing on.

I remembered Aracely's voice on the phone, the tinge of panic, the plea for help. To top it all off, Susan wanted me to go, I had to help her cousin.

It would avail me nothing to turn back now. And so, I pressed the gas pedal instead, driving further into the fog and the uncertain destiny that awaited me.

Just as I was lost in thought, contemplating the seriousness of my upcoming encounter with Aracely and the enigmatic land she now owned, a guttural roar shattered my thoughts.

Out of nowhere, a dark, indescribable shape darted across the road in front of my vehicle. Instinctively, I slammed on the brakes, my tires screeching as I fought to maintain control. I narrowly missed colliding with a gnarled tree that seemed to leap into my path, as if possessed by the same malevolent spirit that haunted these woods.

I allowed a string of profanities to pour out of my mouth as my heart pounded in my chest. I sat there, gripping the wheel, staring into the fog where the creature had vanished. For a moment, it was as if time folded in onto itself. I could not describe the sensation better. I suddenly breathed faster, my skin crawled, my body sweaty.

And then, I was no longer in my car, but standing tall, as a Cherokee warrior armed with a bow and arrow. The forest around me was thicker, untouched by modernity, yet the beast I pursued was the same.

I yelled a fierce whoop at the beast, took aim, drawing the bowstring taut against my cheek. Then, just as quickly, the vision shattered, splintering like a broken mirror and I was back in my car, my fingers white knuckling the steering wheel.

The fog seemed to close in around the vehicle, thicker than before, as if urging me to turn back. But the vision, however unsettling, only strengthened my resolve. There was something deeply wrong here; an ancestral battle left unfinished, and it felt as though it had fallen upon my shoulders to see it through. I could not deny its burden.

I swore again, terror surged through my veins. Taking a deep breath to steady my shaking hands, I pressed down on the gas pedal and continued down the road toward Southland. As I neared the open, rusty gates my phone buzzed, breaking the tense silence that had enveloped the car.

A new message appeared on the screen.

Along with it was a series of photos from Aracely, showcasing footprints—on the walls of her home, but also on the ceilings, imprints of an otherworldly presence she could neither see nor touch. I felt a cold shiver run down my spine, not just from the photos, but from the terse message that accompanied them.

Red Sky, hurry. Something is happening.

But just as I was about to reply, the radio in my car burst to life, blaring native drumming, and chanting so loud that it drowned out all other sounds. It grew louder and louder, drowning out my thoughts, and filling me with a sense of deeper dread that was more palpable than anything I'd felt before.

And then, as suddenly as it had begun, the radio went silent.

But the silence was far worse, for in that void I heard a whispered voice, chillingly close, speaking words in the Cherokee tongue that I understood all too well.

"Beware the Nunnehi."

My hands tightened around the steering wheel.

There was no turning back now.

Chapter Eleven—Aracely

Red Sky's car rolled to a stop on the gravel driveway, each crunch of stone beneath rubber sounded like the ticking of some cosmic clock, counting down, but to what? A resolution, or a further spiraling of mysteries?

I stood on the ancient, creaking porch, half-obscured by an overhanging wisteria whose tendrils seemed to reach for something intangible. Or maybe it reached for me.

What would my mother think about this? If she knew about the footprints, about the horrible feeling here, she'd drag me out of here by the hair of my head.

The weathered boards underfoot groaned, as if empathizing with my jumbled emotions.

The door to his vintage car swung open with a gentle creak, and out stepped Red Sky. He unfolded himself from the driver's seat, a graceful assemblage of long limbs, sculpted features, and the kind of aura that commands both respect and curiosity. The fading sunlight glinted on his dark hair, casting a transient halo that seemed oddly fitting.

Why hadn't Susan mentioned how compelling he was? Yeah, compelling. That's the word I'll go with.

I'd been expecting an older, more solemn figure. Someone wrinkled and gray, the human embodiment of an ancient tome, not a man who looked like he could've just stepped off the pages of a gritty outdoor magazine. He couldn't be much older than me.

My heart performed an unexpected little pirouette, and I chided myself for it.

Really, Aracely? Now?

"Ms. Burkhalter?" His voice was a deep river, flowing smoothly over years of accumulated wisdom and cultural resonance, or so I imagined. His voice could lull the howling spirits themselves into a docile stupor. Again, I was being ridiculous.

"Aracely," I found myself correcting, buoyed by his resonant calm. "Nobody calls me Ms. Burkhalter. That's my mom. Thank you for coming so quickly."

His hand met mine as he offered me a warm handshake. It was both firm and respectful, yet something in the way his eyes met mine made it feel profoundly intimate. I imagined a lingering connection that might've been awkward in another situation, but now just seemed necessary. I believed I could trust him.

Why I believed that, I sure as hell couldn't say.

"May I go inside? Will you show me?" he asked as he lifted his leather satchel, filled with unknown sacred items no doubt, from his shoulder. "I'd like to see the footprints. Was this the first time you've seen anything like this inside the house? What about outside?"

"Of course I'll show you," I agreed, swiveling to lead the way back into the mansion's gaping maw. "I came home once and found all my plants destroyed. There have been other things, too, mostly weird feelings but no moccasin prints. No. I've never seen this. Inside or outside the house. But this fog is weird too. Don't you think?"

He nodded in agreement; his warm brown eyes studied the exterior of the old mansion. As I led the way and crossed the threshold, a shiver of icy anticipation traveled down my spine. The atmosphere inside Southland seemed to congeal, as if awaiting the verdict of this man, this shaman, who had just entered its haunted halls.

Our footsteps whispered through the gloom and I cast a sidelong glance at Red Sky.

Together, we stepped further into the heart of Southland. I didn't have to point out the evidence. It was everywhere. I'd half believed I imagined all this, but I hadn't.

"Is it possible that the Haunted House attraction left these? Perhaps interaction with the atmosphere, the dampness of the fog activated some sort of paint." As he mused his long fingers touched a nearby footprint. He rubbed the footprint and sniffed it. "Nevermind. That's definitely not paint."

I shrugged, but there was no way I was sniffing those footprints to confirm his observation.

"You saged the house recently. I can smell it." Red Sky's gaze flickered, almost imperceptibly, as he took in the space around us. His eyes settled on the oil paintings and dusty curtains and then finally on me.

"Yes," I answered, self-consciously fiddling with the loose threads at the hem of my shirt. *Why did I look like a bum today?* "But as you can see, it didn't exactly work. If anything, the energy in here feels even more...I don't know—turbulent. I mean, I've been trying to do the right thing. Cleaning this place up; making it a place of honor and happiness. It's still a mess, but it was way worse just a few days ago."

Red Sky smiled gently, but didn't share his thoughts immediately. He set his leather satchel down on a worn table that had seen better days. The table was also doomed to land in the burn pile.

"Take me upstairs," he prompted gently. "If you don't mind."

"What?" I asked, startled by his question.

"I'd like to see the rest of the house. If that's okay."

"Oh, duh. Sure. You lead the way," I waved him toward the staircase and followed him. I tried to keep my breathing steady, but I was terrified. I didn't want to be up here. It was as if an invisible person—or something— had claimed it.

We walked up and down the hall, he entered every room. I was relieved to see no footprints, but it did not shake the uneasy feeling I held in the pit of my stomach.

"Saging can often act like a reset button, stirring up energy rather than banishing it. It's possible you've unsettled whatever resides here rather than sending it on its way. Unintentionally, of course. It happens, Aracely."

Ara-cell-lee. I liked the way he said my name.

"Unsettled?" I echoed; my voice tinged with a tremor I couldn't control. "You mean I've made them angry? Ticked off the ghosts, or whatever made these tracks."

He turned to face me, his expression earnest, yet somehow soothing. "Not necessarily angry. From what I have learned, energies, or spirits, have their own frequencies and their own motives. The sage might've acted as a wake-up call. Like a call and response."

I had absolutely no idea what he was talking about. My eyes met his, searching for some inkling of reassurance. "And that's why you're here. You know how to handle this stuff, right? The call and response?"

"I'm here to help as much as I can," he confirmed, his voice imbued with a weight that settled some of the frantic butterflies in my stomach. At least a little. "We'll work together to figure out what's happening at Southland, what these spirits want, and how we can bring peace to this place. We will try. "

Ugh. That doesn't sound too promising.

"And if we can't figure it out?" The question escaped my lips before I could stop it. "What happens then?"

His eyes, dark pools that reflected my own worry, held my gaze for a moment that felt suspended in time. "Then we'll know you've truly awakened something," he finally said, "and we'll have to prepare for what comes next. It may not be the sage, Aracely. It may be your heritage. You are Cherokee, are you not?"

"Half Cherokee," I said as we walked back downstairs.

"How is a person a half anything?" He laughed softly, but it did not feel like mockery. More like a statement of fact—or faith. I couldn't be sure which. "You are, or you are not. You are alive, or you are dead. You are Cherokee, or you are not. Which is it?"

His question hung in the air between us. I had no answer so I shrugged and hoped we could move on. After an extended pause he picked up his leather bag. "I would like to search the grounds. Care to show me around?"

"Sure."

As we stepped off the porch, the air grew thick with an otherworldly fog, wrapping us in a milky haze that seemed to breathe in sync with the land. It was as if Southland itself exhaled this mist, obscuring reality and painting everything in eerie shades of gray.

Our footsteps sounded muffled, each crunch of autumn leaf and snap of dry twig swallowed by the fog as if consumed by some insatiable appetite.

I shivered, even though it wasn't particularly cold.

There was a weight to the atmosphere, as if the mist were saturated with whispers from spirits long gone yet ever-present. Red Sky seemed attuned to this shift, his eyes scanning the landscape like a hawk hunting for something just beyond its line of sight.

With every step, it felt as if we were sinking deeper into an ethereal, unmarked territory. A place where the mundane world met its spectral twin. Would we accidentally step to the other side?

The fog distorted everything, twisting trees into strange shapes, their branches like arms outstretched in a timeless dance, or an eternal curse—I couldn't decide which.

Then Red Sky paused, bending to examine the ground. Through the fog, I could barely make out what caught his attention, but when he straightened up and looked at me, his eyes held a new, unnerving intensity.

"Moccasin tracks," he murmured, his voice tinged with a solemnness that sent a shiver crawling down my spine like a wayward spider. "Just like the ones inside your home. They're fresh too."

The revelation hung heavy between us, mingling with the fog and filling the air with an added density.

These weren't just tracks; they were vestiges, spectral breadcrumbs left behind by entities that defied rational explanation.

In that moment, even the fog seemed to hold its breath, as if awaiting our response to the land's chilling secret.

"The land is awakening," Red Sky finally broke the silence, his words whispered yet reverberating through the still air. "And it doesn't intend to do so quietly."

I froze as my ears pricked up. I heard something. Something odd. Was he hearing it too?
We stood there for a moment, enshrouded in a fog that hid more than it revealed, two souls bound by a mystery as old as the land beneath our feet and as elusive as the mist around us.

Then it was over. Whatever I heard went silent. Or so I believed for a moment.

As we ventured deeper into the land's foggy embrace, a distant sound began to pierce the hushed atmosphere—a rhythmic drumming, low and steady, like a heartbeat.

Tump, tump, tump, tump.

The drumming had a pattern to it, a pattern that repeated. I glanced at Red Sky, realizing that the same sound had caught his attention as well.

His eyes met mine, and in that exchange, unspoken understanding flowed; we were both hearing it, which meant it was real—or as real as anything could be in this surreal landscape.

Compelled by a mixture of fear and fascination, we began walking towards the source of the sound. Each step seemed to draw us deeper into a place that transcended time, where past and present, corporeal, and ethereal, bled into one.

I moaned softly as the drumming grew louder, filling the air with a haunting resonance that seemed to vibrate through the very core of our beings. I didn't mean to make a sound, but the drumming pulled it out of me. *How was that even possible?*

"Careful, Aracely. Watch your step."

Just as I felt we might finally breach the veil and glimpse the drummer, a spine-chilling scream ruptured the air, shredding the dense fog and jolting me to my core. The scream didn't seem human, nor entirely animalistic—it was a wail of sheer agony and anger that transcended description.

Red Sky's fingers closed around mine with an urgency that left no room for doubt.
We broke into a run, the fog swirling angrily around us as if stirred hatefully by our intrusion. We dodged gnarled roots and twisted branches, guided less by sight than by an adrenaline-fueled instinct for survival.

Each of our pounding footfalls seemed to echo the ominous drumming that had first led us astray, as if marking a countdown to an outcome too grim to contemplate. As we neared the house, Southland materialized out of the fog like a ghostly mirage.

Red Sky's Nova sat waiting, an incongruous relic in this timeworn landscape. Without a word, he flung open the passenger door and threw me inside. He raced to the other side and in one fail swoop opened his door, fell in the seat, and slammed the heavy door behind him. Red Sky revved the engine and sped away and I dared a look back.

Through the rearview mirror, the fog seemed to churn in our wake, as if reaching for us with tendrils of ancient resentment. I wondered what we had encountered—what old spirits I had awakened. And if Red Sky was frightened, what chance did I have?

As we left Southland's boundaries, it felt like a defeat rather than a respite. A withdrawal from a battlefield whose combatants were not of this world, but whose scars would be all too real. This was a battle I was going to lose.

Tears flowed down my cheeks and I could do nothing to stop them.

Chapter Twelve–Jack

Sitting in the worn armchair in my living room, I rubbed the fibers of the heirloom blanket—passed down through generations—graze my calloused fingers.

My eyes were drawn to the nearby wall of photographs, each frame captured a snapshot of an almost forgotten happy moment, culminating in the most recent picture of my grandson, Red Sky.

College graduate, anthropologist, and, if the stars aligned right, the next shaman in our lineage. I was still shocked and amazed that he'd agreed to apprentice with me. I could only thank *Unetlanvhi*, the Great Spirit, for his change of heart.

My grandson had no idea of my condition, of the timeline I was working with and I had no intention of telling him.

I would leave before I became too sick. I would not dwindle and die in a poisonous hospital room surrounded by technology. I would leave this earth in the old way. I would take a soul journey and never return.

Red Sky had always been a studious one, more inclined to bury himself in books and theories than to embrace the mysteries of the spirit world. He treated our family's legacy with the same scrutiny as any other subject matter—something to be studied, understood, and perhaps questioned. But to his credit, he was never dismissive, never disrespectful.

He'd earned his degrees, presenting theses and dissertations that would leave most baffled. But what made me prouder was that after years of academic pursuit, he'd finally agreed to sit down and learn the traditions, the rituals, the very essence of what it meant to be a shaman in our family. All of his earnest studying would not satisfy the need within him to connect to the spirit world.

It wasn't academia he was embracing now, but a legacy as old as the wind that whispered through the trees, as sacred as the ground upon which our ancestors had walked.

I knew about the Southland property—its unsettling history steeped in a disquieting blend of fact and legend. I knew because my fathers knew and their fathers before them.

There were truths older than most recorded tales, truths that could haunt a man, even a man trained in scientific objectivity. But I had a feeling, deep in my gut, that this venture would mark a transformative chapter in Red Sky's life. I would never have imagined a day when a shaman would be summoned back to that property, what used to be Cherokee land.

When he called to tell me about his intentions, the hesitation in his voice was palpable. I knew he questioned the sanity of his decision, wondered whether he'd bitten off more than he could chew.

To be honest, I shared those fears. I'd been around long enough to know that some stories aren't just stories, that some legends held a weight of truth that could crush the unprepared. Those old lands of ours had not been stolen from us, we, the Cherokee had abandoned them centuries ago.

I stared out the window, where the outline of the trees stood like sentinels guarding ancient secrets. This was the fork in the road for Red Sky—a trial of not just his skills as an anthropologist, but of his spiritual mettle as a budding shaman.

I reached over to the small wooden table beside my chair and picked up a cluster of sage, turning it slowly in my hands. Closing my eyes, I whispered a prayer to the spirits, asking for protection and guidance for my grandson.

If Southland was where he'd confront the limits of his beliefs, then I could only hope that what emerged on the other side would be a man who truly understood the significance of his heritage—of the fearsome and magnificent legends that were not just stories, but realities waiting to be acknowledged.

As I set down the sage bundle, I sensed a ripple in the fabric of the spiritual world, as if echoing my thoughts and perhaps even assenting to them.

Red Sky was walking a perilous path, and I could only hope he'd come out of it with a newfound respect for the mysteries that our family had guarded for generations.

It was a heavy burden, the mantle of a shaman, but it was also an honor. And as I settled deeper into my chair again, draped in the woven tapestry of our history, I felt sure that if anyone could bear it, it was him.

The rattling of a car needing a major tune up rolled up the driveway. The worrisome sound pulled me out of my introspection. I was glad for the distraction. Inevitably, I had begun pondering the unforgiving reality of my illness and the limitations it would impose on my future for far too long today.

These weren't thoughts I wanted, but they were increasingly unavoidable.

I glanced toward the window, recognizing Rae's rusted-out sedan as it parked. What would bring her here today, especially given the looming shadow that Southland cast over her family?

Oh, yes. That's it.

With a sense of foreboding knotting my stomach, and aching bones, I rose to greet her. I'd rather be standing to greet her then allow her to see me struggle to get out of my chair.

I studied Rae as she stepped out of her car. Her once lovely face was etched with lines of worry and years of hardship. Her eyes, once vivid and full of life, now seemed clouded—much like the sky on a day when you can't quite tell if a storm's coming or not.

Yes, even from here I could see that.

My ability to read others had not faded despite the disease in my bones. I took a deep breath and steadied myself as I waited.

Rae Burkhalter walked toward the cabin, her steps hesitant, as if every footfall were a question she was reluctant to ask. I opened the door before she had a chance to knock. A whiff of the forest air filled the room, mixed with a faint scent of her cheap perfume—some sort of musk, perhaps trying to mask the smell of alcohol that so often clung to her.

"Jack, may I come in? I want to talk to you about Aracely," she said, her voice carrying a brittle urgency that unsettled me further. I suddenly felt pain in my legs, pain so bitter that it nearly took my breath away.

And just like that, the room seemed to darken, as if acknowledging the gravity of what was to come. To me and to Aracely—to us all.

"Come in, Rae," I gestured, my heart heavy with the weight of impending revelations. "You are welcome here."

Guiding Rae through the narrow hallway filled with sepia-toned photographs of ancestors and ritual artifacts, I led her into the kitchen. The air here was rich with the earthy aroma of herbal teas and other remedies that hung in glass jars from wooden racks overhead.

My old, vintage table sat in the middle, a relic that had seen decades of meals, conversations, and countless family gatherings. Its wooden surface, worn by years but lovingly polished, held a palpable energy that intensified the atmosphere. It wasn't worth much monetarily, but this table was a treasure to me.

As we sat down, the creak of the wooden chairs seemed to echo longer than usual, as if even the furniture sensed the tension. The window over the sink framed a view of the encroaching twilight, the failing light imbuing the room with an almost sacred solemnity.

I glanced towards the stove where a kettle sat, its worn spout pointing toward the fading light coming in through the window. "Would you like some tea? Coffee, perhaps?" I offered, aiming to cut through the heaviness that enveloped us.

She looked up, her eyes briefly meeting mine before darting away. "No, thank you, Jack," she said, her voice carrying a frailness I had not heard before. Her refusal was more than just a rejection of a drink; it seemed to accentuate the urgency, the gravity of why she was here.

We were past the point of social niceties. The tension resettled, denser this time, as we returned to the reason we were both sitting at this age-old table.

Rae hesitated, her hands clasping and unclasping in her lap. I waited, each second stretching thin, taut like a wire ready to snap. Finally, she spoke.

"Jack, I'm desperate. I've tried talking to her, but Aracely won't listen. She's stubborn—like her father was," her voice quivered as if on the verge of breaking. "That place, Southland... it's cursed. I fear for her life."

As always Rae had a flair for the dramatic, but at least she was sober today, and honestly, she wasn't wrong. Ty Burkhalter had been a good man, but certainly a strong minded one. It was a shame he'd died so terribly and so young.

The air thickened as her words hung there, each syllable heavy with a mother's dread and a history that both our families had been part of, whether we liked it or not. And in that charged moment, a deep dread settled within me.

Whatever force occupied Southland was neither simple folklore, nor just another tale. It was real, it was restless, and now it was a part of Aracely's life—and, by extension, ours–Red Sky and mine.

Trying to assuage the storm of worry I saw swirling in her eyes, I leaned back in my chair and said, "Rae, I know you're concerned, but Red Sky is determined to help Aracely. He's trained for this—"

Rae interrupted, shaking her head, her eyes narrowing. "Trained? Jack, he's just a boy in the grand scheme of things. Anthropology and textbooks don't prepare you for what's out there, for what's happening on that land. He may know the rituals, the lore, but does he understand the real dangers, the unpredictability of what he's dealing with? My Aracely doesn't really appreciate the danger at all."

Just as I was about to say more, a second car's tires crunched on the gravel outside, its sounds cutting through the thick air between us. Both our heads turned toward the window. We both turned toward the window, our eyes meeting the sight of Red Sky's car pulling up beside the cabin. My breath caught in my chest.

The car came to a halt with an air of urgency, as if they were fleeing something indescribable, something incomprehensible.

Before I could count to ten, the cabin door burst open and in strode Red Sky, his eyes wide, his expression a mix of dread and grim determination. Close on his heels was Aracely, her face pale, her eyes haunted. I felt the atmosphere in the room change instantly, as if charged by their palpable fear.

Rae stood abruptly, her chair scraping loudly against the wooden floor. Her eyes widened as she recognized her own flesh and blood, standing at the threshold of something neither of us fully understood. "Aracely, what are you doing here? What happened?"

"Mom?" Aracely shot back, her voice tinged with a blend of surprise, relief, and a hint of embarrassment.

As it became clear that no one knew what to do, I took the lead. "Please, let's go to the living room. Come inside, Red Sky, Aracely. Close the doors, grandson. Lock them all."

Rae, a forceful arm already wrapped protectively around her daughter, tightened her grip. Her eyes were filled with a terror that clawed at my heart. For a moment, she looked like she might break down, but she held herself together, her love for her daughter armoring her against her fears.

"Come, sit," I gestured to the worn but inviting sofas that adorned our living space, their faded patterns a testament to generations of gatherings just like this—although seldom so charged with a sense of impending doom.

We sat, the four of us forming a makeshift circle, as if the very act could create a sanctuary against the forces that seemed to be closing in.

Rae's eyes were still wide, but now they were fixed on Red Sky, as if pleading for him to give shape to her swirling confusion and dread. I noticed that despite her daughter's general disapproval, she stayed close to her mother on the couch.

Yes, the girl is terrified and so is my grandson.

As Red Sky began to recount the events that had transpired, the room fell into a hush so deep it felt like even the walls were leaning in to listen. The timbers of the cabin seemed to hold their breath, as if fearing the consequences of the truths about to unfold.

"We found moccasin tracks around Southland, Grandfather. On the ceiling, across the walls, everywhere. Not just inside the house," he said, his voice tinged with a gravity that told me he'd crossed some sort of unspoken line between his scientific world and the ancestral lore he'd been skeptical of.

Red Sky looked at me and then at Aracely and her mother. "We were investigating the drumming. We heard drumming. As we got closer to where the sound was coming from, we then heard a scream. A blood-curdling scream—it cut through the air. We ran. We didn't look back until we were inside the car."

"Before that though. In the fog," Aracely chimed in, her voice shaky. "There was something moving in the fog. You could hear a strange sound. I can't even describe it."

A moment of silence stretched out, heavy as a storm cloud, as each of us digested the magnitude of what was happening.

Red Sky cleared his throat, drawing our eyes back to him. He looked at each of us as if measuring how much we could bear to know. Finally, his gaze rested on me.

"There's something else," he began hesitantly. "On my way to Southland, a creature ran across the road in front of me. I've never seen anything like it before. It was... monstrous. I had to slam on the brakes to avoid hitting it. And for a moment—just a brief moment—I had a vision. I was a warrior, and I was chasing this beast through a forest dense with shadows."

The room went unnaturally quiet.

You could almost hear the crackling of the fireplace straining to fill the silence. Rae's eyes widened even more if that was possible. Aracely clutched her mother's arm as if physically holding on to reality.

I looked at my grandson, my flesh and blood, standing on the precipice of a world both wondrous and perilous. I felt a shiver run down my spine. It was a shiver of foreboding, yes, but also one of strange hope.

If the boundaries between the seen and the unseen were truly thinning, then perhaps, just perhaps, we had a chance to mend what was broken. But at what cost?

Red Sky's confession hung in the air like a haunting melody, binding us together in a tale that promised darkness, but perhaps, also a sliver of light.

"As a shaman and elder, it's my duty to consult with the others about these developments," I declared, breaking the lingering silence. "We need collective wisdom to navigate through this. The *nunnehi* have made their presence known and you, Aracely, have stirred their curiosity."

Rae shot up from her chair, as if propelled by some invisible force. "Aracely, you're coming with me. I can't leave you there. You can't go back!"

Aracely looked at her mother, her eyes unyielding. "Please calm down. I must go back, Mom. I have to find out what's happening at Southland. Everything I own is tied up in that place. I can't just run away."

I didn't say what I was thinking. *But you did just run away. Fast and far.*

"And who told you to do that, Aracely! You should have talked to me before you bought that place. I could have told you; anyone could have told you. Why? Why would you do this? You wasted what your father left us!"

"Left me, Mom! Left me! You drank up what he left you!"

Aracely was on her feet now, both the women uncaring about the unwanted energy they were releasing in my home. I glanced at my grandson and thankfully he picked up on my concern.

Red Sky interjected, "When she goes back, I'll go with her, Rae. She will not be alone. I promised to help Aracely cleanse the place, I will see it through."

Aracely's mother was not pleased with this proposal. Rae's eyes welled up with tears as she clutched her purse tightly against her chest. "Please, reconsider this madness. I get that you're mad at me, child. Maybe I deserve your anger, but you should not be there. No one should! Tell her, Jack! Tell her the truth!"

Aracely's body stiffened. She wasn't going to back down, clearly. "Despite what you think, Mom, I can fix this. This is my problem. Not yours. And I am no child. I haven't been for a long time. You made sure of that."

Rae's mouth worked, but she said nothing. Instead, she stared at her daughter and yanked her purse up on her slender shoulder. Rae's body shook as she turned away, stepping out into the darkening evening. The screen door creaked behind her, a mournful lament that seemed to echo her sentiments.

I had no doubt she was about to crawl into yet another bottle, but what could one do about that? Red Sky went to the door, closed and locked it again.

"Fine, you two can return, but not today and not without protection. And what protections I have will only keep the nunnehi at bay for a short time, so be mindful of the shadows. If they begin to gather inside the house, get out. Get out before it is too late. If they overpower you, you will not escape."

Moving toward an intricately carved wooden chest, I opened it to reveal bundles of herbs, small amulets, and other ritualistic items. I took out two leather pouches, filling each with a mixture of sage, cedar, and other herbs, along with a small crystal.

Such weak things, but I was confident that they would do the trick. At least in the interim. I hoped the elders would have better solutions than what I could currently offer, medicine pouches.

"Carry these with you. They are amulets of protection, infused with prayers and intention.

They may help shield you from what lurks in those fog-ridden acres. You will know this, Red Sky."

Red Sky nodded, taking the pouch with the somberness of someone accepting a military assignment. Aracely did the same, her fingers trembling ever so slightly as she took the small leather pouch from me.

We all stood there, each absorbed in our thoughts, united yet isolated in our worries and expectations. What would come next was a path shrouded in mists of uncertainty, but one we were now bound to walk, whether by destiny or by folly.

"Stay here for a while. I will go see my brothers. Red Sky, you and Aracely prepare dinner, but no meat. Nothing with blood. I will return soon."

I did not wait for their answer. I walked to the door, paused at the coat rack to retrieve my favorite jacket and hat. I was always cold these days, cold in my bones, but now it was worse.

This cold was not merely from the disease that ravaged my body but from the gathering rage of the nunnehi.

As I stepped outside, I knew the truth. This battle would sap my remaining life.

I can't say why, but that thought saddened me. Why? What else did I have to live for? My beloved wife died more than twenty years ago and my son had moved away a long time ago. Only Red Sky remained and I was not strong enough to truly help him.

I did not cry, but I experienced a strange sort of emptying. A strange sort of fading.

Soon I would fade into nothing.

"So be it," I whispered to the Great Spirit as I climbed into my truck and left my home.

Let the emptying begin.

Chapter Thirteen—Jack

The drive to see my brothers took me through roads that had long ceased to be familiar, though I had traveled them countless times before. A shroud of mist hung over the landscape, dense trees lining the narrow path as if guarding long-forgotten secrets.

My old truck's headlights barely cut through the fog, illuminating patches of gnarled roots and fallen leaves. It was as if nature itself was cautioning me, the obscurity reflecting the uncertainty that tingled at the back of my mind.

I know they will be gathering. I can feel their collective power in my bones. My sick, diseased bones.

Perhaps that knowing wasn't so supernatural. The brothers always gathered near the full moon.

I finally arrived at the timeworn cabin where my brothers gathered—a circle of Cherokee elders, guardians of ancestral wisdom. The air was thick with the scent of sage and cedar as I stepped inside, immediately catching sight of Rae's uncle, a stern figure sitting in the half-light, eyes like embers in the dusk.

My brothers were already seated, their faces etched with lines that told stories of years filled with joys and sorrows, triumphs, and tragedies.

As I joined them, the weight of our collective knowledge and the seriousness of the task ahead filled the room, stifling even the whisper of the wind outside. I hadn't intended to come but here I was, reporting for duty. A few of the brothers gently grunted a welcome at me.

We were about to discuss matters that we hadn't dared to speak of in decades—the signs, the omens, and the whispering echoes of the past that pointed to the return of the nunnehi.

And as I investigated the faces of these men, my lifelong companions in spiritual stewardship, I knew that no words needed to be exchanged for us to understand. The looming shadows of ancient threats were once again stretching their fingers toward the world of men.

My grandson, Red Sky, should be here but I had not invited him—neither had the other elder. Deep down, I wanted to protect him still. How ashamed I should be after all my preaching to him; my encouragement to face the unknown.

As I settled into the circle, my brother, Rae's uncle, Waya, began to speak first. His voice was gravelly, aged by decades of chanting prayers and incantations.

"Brother, come. Have a seat. You are welcome here. Two nights ago, I heard it—the drumming that comes from nowhere and everywhere. The beat of the sacred spirits, our ancestors' songs have come alive again."

Adahy nodded solemnly. "I have seen the animals act in ways they should not. Deer running in circles until they drop of exhaustion, birds flying backward, fish swimming to the surface and gasping for air. There is no doubt that the spirit world wants to warn us of what is to come."

Another brother chimed in, his eyes more piercing than ever. "Even the skies bear witness. A flock of crows formed the shape of the sacred spiral over the river, circling for an hour before dispersing. The water levels in the sacred lake have dropped overnight."

Finally, Atohi, spoke up. "I have felt it in the earth itself. The soil is restless, like the stirrings of a dreamer about to wake. The roots of the ancient trees are shifting, as if trying to pull themselves free."

Each revelation hung in the air, building a tapestry of dread that was all too real. These were not just mere occurrences, not when woven together. They painted a larger picture—one of ancient spirits and half-forgotten horrors--the *nunnehi*.

As the room absorbed the weight of our observations, the flickering firelight seemed to dim, casting dancing shadows that played tricks on the eye.

We all knew the implications of what we were facing. It was a tapestry woven from the oldest stories and the most haunting legends—those that we had hoped would remain nothing but tales to caution the young.

But as the elders shared these signs, a chill, separate from the night air outside, settled among us. We were no longer dealing with stories. We were confronting a reality that none of us, despite our years and wisdom, truly felt prepared for.

A heaviness descended upon the room, thicker than the smoke of a ceremonial fire. It was Waya who broke the silence.

"Jack, your grandson, Red Sky, has taken up the task at Southland. Is he prepared for this? Does he understand what he is walking into? He is new to his path. Although chosen, he is untried. Unblooded."

I felt a knot tighten in my stomach, a clash of emotions wrestling within me. Pride and assuredness of my grandson's bravery and resolve, but there was also fear for Red Sky's inexperience in matters that our people haven't dealt with for generations.

Waya was speaking the truth and I could not deny it.

"Red Sky is educated and strong," I said, forcing steadiness into my voice. "He has learned much in college about anthropology, our history, our culture. He's also taken steps to understand shamanism, our family trade. It is in his blood."

Waya frowned at my answer. "But has he faced the nunnehi? No, none of us have. What makes you think he will push back the darkness?"

Adahy questioned, his eyes narrowing with concern. "Has he confronted any spirits? Must less those who can slip between the fabric of worlds, who have existed since the times our ancestors danced beneath the same moon and stars?"

"He hasn't," I admitted, my words as heavy as stones. "Brothers, of a truth, that worries me. He's strong, but untested in the ways that might matter most now. Why has the land, come to life again? Why have the nunnehi returned? That is the larger question. We must know what they want from us."

Uwohali sighed, his gaze distant as if trying to see through the murk of what lay ahead. "If they are as malevolent as our history suggests, then Red Sky will need more than courage and intellectual knowledge. He will need the wisdom that comes only through experience—experience he doesn't yet have. Yes, why have they returned? We must know this."

Each word spoken was like a thorn, pricking at my soul.

My grandson, for all his promise and intelligence, was stepping into a world far older and darker than any one of us could describe. And as much as I wanted to think otherwise, the air in the room seemed to grow colder with the acknowledgment of his—and our—vulnerability. And our lack of understanding, even after all these centuries.

The nunnehi continued to be elusive and bent on destruction, our destruction.

The flicker of the room's dim lights seemed to cast momentarily deeper shadows, as if underlining the gravity of our conversation. It was Tsuwa, a wizened elder who had rarely spoken throughout the gathering, who cleared his throat to speak.

"Jack, it was not only your decision, but that of the entire tribe, to place Red Sky as our chief shaman. We all saw something in him, a spark perhaps not yet fully kindled, but strong nonetheless. How could we know that the nunnehi would rise at this time? Do you regret the choice now, seeing the path he must step on?"

My eyes met each of theirs in turn.

Old friends and respected elders, their faces etched with the wisdom and concerns of years spent navigating both the spiritual and earthly challenges of our people.

"No, I do not regret it," I responded, my voice tinged with both conviction and vulnerability. "Red Sky has a role to play, a destiny that ties into the wellbeing of our tribe. It's a heavy burden for one so young, yet it's his to carry. But it is also our responsibility to guide him, to arm him with as much wisdom and preparation as we can."

The room absorbed my words, each elder pondering their weight. Adahy spoke up. "Then we must stand behind our decision, behind him, despite the risks and the worry that gnaws at our hearts. But we can't ignore that the girl, Aracely, is also a part of this. She is key here. What do we know about her?"

I sighed, leaning back into my chair. I had to remind the elders of the truth, even if Waya was reluctant to do so. "She is of the lineage of Keta, though she knows little of her heritage, or her potential role in all this. She's untrained, but there's something about her—a kind of raw, unshaped power—that can't be ignored. She is Rae's daughter, a Cherokee, brothers."

I let that sink in. Waya, Rae's uncle, Aracely's great uncle nodded in agreement.

"We've placed immense responsibility on the shoulders of the young and inexperienced," Uwohali mused. "It's a gamble of fates, a roll of the bones, brothers. Yet, perhaps it's time for a new generation to confront the old ghosts and emerge from the other side, either as heroes or warnings for the generations that come after."

The room went quiet, each of us contemplating the precipice we stood upon—a cliff's edge between tradition and evolution, the known and the unknown, life and death. Waya's voice finally broke the silence. His voice had a melodic quality, soothing yet stern, like a lull in the storm that warns you to brace for what's coming.

"Jack, you say the girl is untrained. And yet, she is of Keta's lineage. You know what our ancestors have spoken of—that one day a seer will rise from that line. A seer that will correct the Great Wrong. Do you think she's the one?"

I felt a heavy sigh escape my lungs as I met his penetrating gaze. "It's a possibility we cannot ignore, Waya. She's already shown a sensitivity to the spiritual world, whether she understands it or not. But she's vulnerable, especially without proper guidance. It could be that the nunnehi have arisen because she has taken possession of the land."

Adahi's eyes widened. "Yes, that must be it. The truth has been before us yet we have not seen it. The nunnehi expect the Cherokee to serve them once more."

"And what does your grandson make of her?" inquired Uwohali, his eyes sharp like flint. "Does Red Sky understand her importance, her potential role in all of this?"

"I think he's beginning to," I admitted. "Red Sky is perceptive, but there's a fine line between recognizing a gift and knowing how to wield it. That goes for both of them."

Tsula leaned forward, his hands clasped tightly, "Then you must guide them, Jack. This burden falls heavily upon your shoulders, whether you welcome it or not. We understand why you have stepped back, but you must return and see this through. We will stand with Red Sky."

They all nodded and murmured words of agreement. Yes, the brothers knew about my illness, but at my request, they spoke not of it. Not to anyone. It was a secret, but clearly not one that I would be able to keep forever.

"I intend to and I thank you for your help," I assured them, "but we should all be prepared for what that entails. The nunnehi have been dormant, but they are not weakened. And they will not take kindly to any attempts to thwart their return."

Uwohali nodded gravely. "Then you must lead us, as you always have. But heed our words, Jack. If Red Sky and Aracely are not prepared for what they're facing, then it won't just be their lives at stake, but the soul of our tribe, perhaps even the world as we know it."

The weight of his words settled over me like a mantle, heavy and inescapable. I looked around the room at the faces of my brothers, weathered maps of life and wisdom, and felt the resolve harden within me.

"I will guide them," I declared. "And may the Great Spirit be with us all."

"Asitaga, you've been quiet," I observed, turning my gaze toward the youngest of my spiritual brothers. His name meant 'Warrior,' but in many ways, he was a contemplative soul, prone to deep thoughts and longer silences.

Finally, he spoke, his voice imbued with an edge of urgency that belied his usual calm.

"Free will is a powerful force, and it can either be our greatest ally, or most unpredictable foe. The young ones must freely accept this task. They must know what they are facing. Truly know."

I nodded. "I understand. Red Sky and Aracely have their own minds, their own fears and hopes. We can guide, but we cannot dictate. I will be sure they know."

"And if the girl chooses to walk away?" Waya asked, locking eyes with me. "What if the burden proves too great for her, or for Red Sky? The only other one is Rae and she is not fit to fight the nunnehi." A hush fell over the room. The question hung in the air like an unspoken curse, laden with implications we all understood, but dreaded to articulate.

"I hope it doesn't come to that," I finally said. "But if it does, we'll face that reality when we arrive at it. Until then, we guide, we guard, and we hope. We must have faith."

"We hope for the best," echoed Asitaga, the finality in his voice serving as a solemn amen to a prayer we all silently shared.

"It is decided then," I summed up, feeling the weight of the gathering lift ever so slightly. "I'll help them—we shall help them--as best as we can, prepare them for the trials ahead. We must be vigilant, all of us. The veil between our world and that of the nunnehi is thinning. We need to fortify it, to safeguard what we hold dear." I continued, "If we fail, we fail fighting, brothers. As did our ancestors."

Waya agreed, "Aracely is special, not just as a person, but as a seer. Like her mother once was. She's the last of her lineage, unless she has a child of her own. If the nunnehi are returning, she's the key. Her blood could be our guiding star."

"Or our undoing," interjected Tsula, his weathered face etched with lines of worry that seemed to deepen with each spoken word. "Visionaries see, but they do not always understand. It's a gift fraught with peril and she is untrained."

I looked around the room at my brothers--wise men who had traversed the spiritual realms, who had sung down the moon and whispered secrets to the wind.

"I know the risks," I admitted. "And that's why I intend to stand beside her and Red Sky as they walk this path. I may be old, and my time draws near, but I still have strength to lend, wisdom to share." The room fell silent, each of us lost in our own thoughts, pondering the many possible futures that branched out from this point in time.

We knew the stakes were high, higher perhaps than any challenge our tribe had faced in centuries. But there was no turning back now. The die had been cast, and all we could do was wait and watch as the events unfolded, carrying us along on a current that seemed as relentless as it was unpredictable.

"Then it's settled," I finally said, rising to my feet, my voice tinged with a gravity I hadn't felt in years. "I'll go home and prepare them. We have a long road ahead." With a solemn nod from each, we knew our meeting had come to an end. I turned to leave, my steps echoing in the silent room, each footfall a reminder of the dire path we were now committed to tread.

My bones hurt, they ached, but I could not listen to their complaints. I had one last task to accomplish.

I left the meeting cabin, its wooden structure seemingly fading into the surrounding forest, as if nature itself conspired to keep our meeting a secret. The air outside felt colder than when I arrived, the wind carrying whispers from the unseen.

For a moment, I stood there, allowing the gravity of the evening's conversation to fully sink in.

A lone howl broke the silence, far off, but close enough to stir the hairs on the back of my neck. "The nunnehi," I muttered under my breath. Whether it was a coyote or something far more ancient didn't matter; the land was speaking, and its message was clear.

Danger was brewing, an old storm reawakening, and my grandson, Red Sky, along with Aracely, were standing at its epicenter.

I opened the door of my truck and climbed in, gripping the steering wheel as if I could navigate away from the impending storm. But some storms, I knew, must be faced head-on. I started the engine and began the drive back home, each mile taking me closer to a fate that felt increasingly sealed, yet fluid enough to defy predictions.

It was a paradox, like walking through a mist that could either cool your skin or freeze your bones.

I tightened my grip on the steering wheel, a sense of urgency spurring me on. Could I prepare them in time? Did I have enough wisdom to guide them through a maze with walls that kept shifting? As my truck's headlights cut through the encroaching darkness, I couldn't shake the sensation of invisible eyes watching me.

Was it the nunnehi, those elusive spirits of the land? Or was it the weight of my brothers' words settling in, casting their own kind of shadow?

A flock of crows took off from a nearby tree as I passed, a sudden eruption of dark wings and cawing voices that sounded like a judgment, a verdict delivered from the natural world.

The truck bumped over the gravel as I pulled into my driveway. The front porch light was on, casting a warm glow that cut through the night's tension.

Normally, that light would bring comfort, a symbol of home and safety. Tonight, it felt like a beacon, drawing me back into the storm I'd just left.

Taking a deep breath, I killed the engine and stepped out, my boots crunching on the gravel. I looked up at the sky, half expecting to see some omen, a comet, or a sudden flash of lightning to punctuate the evening. But all I saw were stars, twinkling indifferently to the drama that unfolded beneath them.

How odd. Didn't the earth know that evil had come upon it?

I walked up to the front door and paused, hand hovering over the doorknob. On the other side were Aracely and Red Sky, young but no longer naive, awaiting guidance from a man who himself was grappling with questions that had no easy answers.

I turned the knob and stepped inside.

Whatever awaited us, we would face it together armed with the fragile, but unyielding strength of a lineage that had endured countless storms and would endure still.

And so, bracing myself for the unknown, I took a deep breath.

Chapter Fourteen—Aracely

The air felt heavy with an electric tension as Red Sky and I sat across from each other at the small, worn wooden table. I couldn't believe the attraction I felt for him. It really wasn't like me to be a slave to my desires.

Not that I was behaving like a tramp. But my thought life was disturbing. No make that surprising.

The room was dimly lit, with only the overhead light casting an ethereal glow that danced upon the aging wood and our faces. The table was set meticulously with an arrangement of vegetarian dishes: a bowl of quinoa speckled with herbs, a platter of fire-roasted vegetables glistening in olive oil, and a stir-fry of colorful bell peppers that added a vibrant touch to the otherwise somber setting.

Every dish had been carefully prepared, mostly by Red Sky, yet something was conspicuously missing. The absence hung in the air, filling the room with a silent question that finally escaped my lips.

"Why no meat?" I inquired, my eyes meeting his as I gently stirred the quinoa on my plate. "Why that instruction? Is this a religious thing?"

Red Sky looked up, his eyes locking onto mine as if he had been waiting for this question. The light flickered in his eyes, making them seem even more mysterious and deep.

"It's a form of fasting," he explained softly, his voice carrying the weight of traditions and beliefs that I knew little about. My mother never talked to me about such things. In her mind, I was not true Cherokee. As if I'd asked to be born of a white father.

Red Sky heaped quinoa on my plate. "In times of spiritual importance, avoiding meat helps to cleanse the body and focus the mind. It's part of our preparation, you could say."

The words hung in the air, mixing with the scent of the herbs and vegetables, creating an atmosphere that felt like a bridge between the material and the mystical. My fork hovered over the plate, suddenly imbued with a significance that went beyond a simple meal.

It was as if, by partaking in this food, I was crossing into a realm that Red Sky already occupied—a realm that was both fascinating and unnerving.

I tilted my head, curiosity getting the better of me. "You sound like you're preparing us for an actual battle." That was meant to sound like a joke, but it sounded hollow.

Thankfully, he chuckled, a sound that somehow managed to be both light and laden with complexity. "Well, in a way, I am. But it's not the kind of battle you're thinking of. The tools won't be guns or knives, but ancient rites and a clear mind."

"And you really believe that not eating meat will help?" I smiled in between bites of food. It was quite delicious.

A shadow seemed to pass over his face, like a cloud momentarily obscuring the sun. He paused, as if wrestling with some inner debate.

Yes, I could see the gears turning, the anthropologist in him questioning, analyzing. Yet, there was something else—a deeper, more instinctual part of him that moved beyond logic, into a territory that science couldn't easily chart. I hungered to possess the same passion he held.

"You could say I'm hedging my bets," he finally said, the corners of his mouth turning up in a hesitant smile. "Science has its limits, so does tradition. If we're dealing with something as unexplained as what's happening at Southland, I want every advantage I can get."

His words reverberated in the dim room, filled with the relics and talismans of generations long gone.

It felt like an echo, a call to something ancient that existed within us, whether we understood it or not. And in that moment, I knew that the chasm between his scientific skepticism and his shamanic heritage was a tightrope that Red Sky was still learning to navigate.

I respected him for that. He was certainly miles ahead of me in that regard.

The sound of the front door creaked open and broke our conversation. Heavy footsteps approached, signaling the return of Grandfather Jack. He entered the room, the lines on his face deepened, as if etched by the weight of some unseen knowledge.

"I have been to see my brothers," he began, pausing to study each of our faces. There was a gravity in his eyes I hadn't seen before, like a storm gathering force, but not yet breaking.

"And?" Red Sky leaned forward, a subtle tension gripping his body.

"They have agreed to help us. They acknowledge the signs, the whispers on the wind, the footprints in the earth—and in your home. These signs can no longer be ignored. It is clear that the shadows have returned."

I caught a fleeting glance between grandfather and grandson. Something unspoken passed between them, a hidden layer to the conversation that I couldn't quite grasp.

"What did they say, Grandfather?" Red Sky's voice was lower now, tinged with both respect and urgency.

Jack paused, choosing his words carefully. "They believe that what is happening at Southland is a manifestation of old, very old, powers. Forces we haven't dealt with for generations."

"And the nunnehi?" I asked, unable to contain my curiosity. 'What do they want?"

Jack sighed, deeply. "They are more than legend, more than bedtime stories to scare children. And whether we are ready or not, we might have to face them." I noticed he did not answer my question. Should I ask him again?

"Did they offer any advice, any guidance?" Red Sky's question filled the room, laden with a hope for some form of direction.

Jack looked squarely at his grandson. "They will lend their knowledge, their power. You won't face this alone, Red Sky. But remember, what lies ahead requires more than just the wisdom of elders. It will demand something from each of us that we might not be prepared to give."

The atmosphere in the room was heavy, but not oppressive, as we settled around the small wooden table to share a meal. The empty place setting had been prepared for Jack before he arrived. The plates filled with vegetables, grains, and aromatic herbs were passed to him silently, each of us absorbed in our own thoughts.

Finally, Jack broke the silence. "Aracely, I would like you to stay the night here with us. I know you are eager to return to Southland, but you must understand—the land requires proper respect and preparation before we step onto it again. They know who you are, Aracely. They know you are Cherokee."

His words hung in the air, like the final notes of a somber melody. I looked from Jack to Red Sky, who nodded in agreement, his eyes communicating an unspoken depth of understanding and concern.

"They know? How do they know?" I asked, feeling alarmed. I set down my fork and pushed the plate away.

"These creatures, they smell you. They know your blood." Jack frowned sadly, his eyes reflecting a blend of worry and paternal warmth.

"We will all go back in the morning, fortified and ready for whatever awaits us."

Oh my God. They can smell me? Why? How?

With that, we quietly finished our meal, each in our own cocoon of reflection and anticipation. I did not voice my questions. Instead, I helped clean up the kitchen, showered and prepared to rest. As I retreated to the cozy, makeshift bed on the couch, Jack handed me an additional warm blanket. I noticed that Red Sky carefully avoided me. He wouldn't even meet my eyes.

"Sleep as much as you can, Aracely. Tomorrow will challenge us all." Jack said warmly before he shuffled off to his room at the back of the cabin.

As I closed my eyes, the events of the day played like a vivid tapestry of interwoven fates. And for the first time in a long while, I felt as if I was part of something much larger than myself—a tapestry that included the history of lands, the wisdom of elders, and the courage to face an uncertain future.

I am Cherokee. I belong. It is not as my mother said. I am not cast off. I am wanted and loved.

The couch was comfortable enough, wrapped in a blanket that smelled of sage and cedar, but sleep remained elusive.

Two nights in a row of sleeping on couches. At least this one did not smell like cigarettes.

Still, I sighed in frustration.

I could hear the subtle sounds of the night—the distant call of an owl, the rustle of leaves as a night breeze swept through the forest. And above it all, a gentle creak of the cabin door that seemed to echo through my bones.

Red Sky went outside. I knew it was him as clearly as I knew my own name. I waited. For a few minutes, then half an hour. I could plainly see the clock on the wall beside me. Was he not going to return?

Quietly, I slipped out of the blanket and tiptoed toward the door, careful not to wake Jack. I changed my mind and wrapped the blanket around my shoulders to protect my body from the cool night air. I hadn't brought a jacket with me as I had not prepared to stay here.

The cool night air embraced me as I stepped out, carrying the scents of pine and damp earth. I followed a faint trail of light, a luminescent thread woven by the moon and stars, that led me to him.

Red Sky sat alone, in front of a small fire.

The flames cast flickering shadows on his face, revealing a visage in quiet contemplation. He was looking up, lost in the celestial tapestry of the moon and stars that adorned the night sky.

"Couldn't sleep?" His voice was soft, almost a whisper, but it pierced the stillness like a flint striking steel. He hadn't even turned to look at me.

Well, he must have heard me. I was not an expert at sneaking up on people.

"I could ask you the same question," I replied, taking a cautious step closer.

He gestured for me to sit beside him on the wooden bench. "I find nights like these grounding, especially when life spirals into uncertainty. The sky—so vast and eternal— makes my problems seem smaller in comparison."

As I settled next to him, our hands inadvertently touched, sending an electric charge through me. For a moment, the world seemed to hold its breath. I quickly moved my hand although that was the last thing I wanted to do.

"You know," he finally said, his voice tinged with vulnerability, "I'm often caught between two worlds. My education as an anthropologist pulls me toward logic, reason. Yet, my lineage, my training as a shaman, pulls me toward things that most people would dismiss as myths or superstitions. Like you, I am caught between two worlds, Aracely. It is a difficult place to be, is it not?"

I looked at him, his face now illuminated by both the fire and the moonlight and felt a strange sense of intimacy and understanding.

"It is difficult, but it is not impossible to navigate. At least, that is my hope. Maybe it's not about choosing one world over the other, but about finding a balance, a harmony between them. For both of us."

He smiled, and for the first time, I saw a glimmer of peace in his eyes. "I'm glad you're here, Aracely. We're walking this path together, aren't we?"

"Yes," I whispered, feeling the weight of our joined fates, "we are."

As we sat there, side by side in the embrace of the night, gazing at the moon as if it held all the answers, I felt a complex tapestry of emotions weaving itself around us—fear, hope, uncertainty, but most of all, a sense of unity in facing whatever lay ahead.

And in that moment, under the moon's ancient, watchful eye, it felt like enough.

Chapter Fifteen—Jack

The morning mist still clung to the earth as I drove through the winding roads that led to Rae's house. Every bump and jolt of the car seemed to echo in my aching bones, a painful reminder of time's relentless march and my own personal battle. I'd risen early. Earlier than Red Sky and Aracely who were sleeping in my grandson's bed.

Well, if they'd found comfort in one another's arms, who was I to put my mouth to it?

I moaned with pain but forced myself to push the discomfort aside. Today was not about me; it was about Rae. About urging her to embrace a destiny she had long tried to elude.

I parked the car and approached her front door, pausing for a moment to steady my trembling hands. The yard was cluttered around her trailer. A pitiful example of her true worth. Her true self. How had she so lost her way?

When I knocked, the door swung open almost instantly, as if she'd been waiting just beyond it. Rae's eyes met mine, bloodshot and heavy with something unspoken.

"Rae. May I come in?" I asked, swallowing the lump that had formed in my throat.

"Is this about Aracely? Is she okay?"

"So far. Yes."

Rae stepped aside, her gaze dropping to the floor as she gestured for me to enter. I was surprised that she granted me entrance with no further argument.

The atmosphere inside Rae's home felt heavy, almost stifling, as if weighed down by the emotional debris of years gone by.

Mismatched furniture occupied the space, each piece like a relic of a different phase of her life—none of them seeming to belong together, much like the woman herself. The scent of stale alcohol permeated the air, competing with the lingering aroma of incense, a failed attempt to cleanse the environment, perhaps.

As I walked further in, my shoes contacted a worn-out rug, its pattern barely discernible, dulled by time and neglect. Rays of morning sunlight managed to pierce through the gaps in the heavy curtains, casting fragmented pools of light that seemed to hesitate before touching the floor.

Dust particles floated aimlessly in these shafts of light, like lost souls seeking a path. Like the lost soul that lived here.

Rae, how had this happened to you? The tribe's rejection of Ty, of your union did more damage than anyone could have predicted. I warned Waya not to treat you so harshly but my advice was not heeded. Well, the point was moot now.

The walls were adorned with framed pictures, images of happier times frozen for eternity, each telling its own silent story.

Rae led me to the living room, her movement sluggish, almost as if she were walking through a viscous fluid. The fatigue and despair that seemed to radiate off her were almost palpable. She gestured for me to sit on a faded sofa, its cushions sagging, seemingly as drained of life as she was. As I lowered myself onto it, a cloud of dust billowed into the air, each particle an unsettled fragment of the past.

I thought of Rae's mother, how joyful she'd been when Rae had been born.

What would she think now that her daughter was daily drinking herself to death?

The room felt smaller with both of us in it, the air thickening with unsaid words and unacknowledged truths. She finally broke the silence, her voice tinged with a bitterness that could have only been fermented over years.

"What do you want from me, Jack? Aracely would not have sent you. My daughter hates me."

And so we began.

Rae reached for the half-empty bottle of whiskey on the coffee table, its amber contents glowing ominously in the fractured light. Her hand wavered for a moment, as though questioning the decision. But finally, she unscrewed the cap and poured a generous amount into a stained glass, half-filled with melting ice.

I said nothing to her about it. What was there to say that she had not already heard?

She took a gulp, her eyes closing momentarily as the liquid coursed through her veins, the burning sensation providing a fleeting escape from her emotional turmoil. Or so I imagined. Did it really do any good?

But as she leaned back into her chair, her eyes like daggers as she stared into space, I felt a wave of pain wash over me.

It was a piercing agony that seemed to shoot from my spine and flood every inch of my being. I grimaced involuntarily, clutching the armrests of the sofa for support, my knuckles turning white. The room began to swim before my eyes, the ceiling, the walls, and the floor blurring into an indistinct mass.

It was one of those episodes again, an agonizing reminder of the disease that was steadily chipping away at my vitality. I knew I was going to die, but I prayed it would not be today. I had too much to do before I left the physical world.

When I managed to regain my focus, I found Rae staring at me with widened eyes, the glass of whiskey suspended in mid-air.

The nurse in her had snapped to attention, her professional instincts momentarily overriding her alcohol-induced haze. Her eyes met mine, and I saw a flicker of realization there—the gravity of my condition sinking in.

"Jack, you don't look well," she said, her voice suddenly devoid of its earlier bitterness. "What is going on? Is it your blood pressure? I have a cuff. Let me get my kit."

"Don't bother. It will pass."

Rae set the glass down on the table, her hand trembling slightly. "What do you mean?" She looked at me, her eyes now clear, searching for meaning.

I took a moment to observe her. *Yes, I could see her clearly now. Thanks to the Great Spirit, the moment passed.*

"I am sick, Rae. That is all I will say on the matter."

Time and struggle had etched lines on her face, evidence of experiences that had stolen the smoothness of her skin, but not the depth of her eyes. Her hair once vibrant still rebellious in its waves, had strands of gray weaving through it like melancholic poetry.

She was no longer the youthful beauty who had first captivated the tribe, and yet, her essence remained undeniable.

"Rae," I began again, my voice heavy, but sincere. "You've been running away for too long. From your responsibilities, your gifts, and ultimately, from yourself. You are a visionary, a seer, by birthright, a woman with a powerful lineage. The tribe, your family, your daughter—they all need you to be who you are meant to be."

My eyes met hers, and for a moment, I saw the woman she could still become. I had always admired her, even at her lowest, during her battles with the bottle. Her spirit, though submerged, was never fully extinguished. It flickered like a stubborn flame, refusing to be snuffed out, casting intermittent light on the walls of her self-imposed prison.

She sighed, dropping her gaze to the floor, as if the weight of my words was too much for her to bear. Then, lifting her eyes back to mine, she spoke.

"They rejected me, Jack. I loved Ty. He did everything they asked of him. He endured the tests, took on our tribe's mantle and yet, they hated him. They hated my daughter—and me. Why should I go back?"

I sighed as I considered her truth. Yes, it was true. I had seen the tribe's rejection firsthand. I should have done more, but it had been a different time. A less tolerant time. I told her so, but it did not soothe her bitterness.

"You have every right to reject them, to avoid the tribe but your daughter needs you. She needs her mother, the seer. I will speak frankly then. Aracely's blood—Keta's blood has awakened the nunnehi. They have come because again, one of Cherokee blood has claimed the land and none other than the blood that first summoned them. They want her to serve them and be of service to her. Do you know what that means?"

Rae rose from her chair and slammed down her glass, splashing whiskey all over the table. "That cannot be! Aracely is only half blood. She is not Cherokee. Her blood would not be enough to call them back!"

It was my turn to slap the table. "Damn it, Rae! The very prejudice you experienced you inflict on your own daughter! Your words have power! You know this."

Rae plunked back down in her wooden chair. "I wanted to protect her, Jack. That's all I have ever wanted to do. When Ty died, I couldn't protect her anymore. I had to make her see the truth. I had to protect her from their hate. It is better than she is not Cherokee!"

"They never hated her, Rae. Nor did they hate you. They were ignorant and short sighted. Most of them know that now. And here we are. It is you that can save the tribe. You can save Aracely! Only you. If you do not crawl out of the bottle and take control of your bitterness she will be consumed. Come with me to see the elders. Hear what they have to say before you drown yourself completely."

Rae began to sob. I did not offer her any comfort. She had been babied long enough. I meant every word I said to her. I found a box of tissues and handed them to her. When she was finished crying, she pulled out a few tissues and wiped her face.

"Alright, Jack. I'll go see the elders. Only for Aracely. What's our next step?"

A small, almost imperceptible smile curled at the corners of my mouth.

The path ahead was perilous and uncertain, but for the first time in years, I sensed a glimmer of hope. I moved towards the kitchen, with a newfound strength seeping into my bones, and started brewing some coffee.

Rae would need to be sober for the journey ahead, a journey that could redefine us both.

"I hate coffee," she said with a sad smile.

"Yet you have some." Pouring the freshly brewed coffee into a cup, I handed it to Rae. She wrapped her fingers around the mug. She took a slow sip, her eyes closing momentarily as if to savor this simple, earthly pleasure.

"Thank you, Jack," she said softly, setting the mug back onto the table. "I'll get dressed. Just give me a few minutes."

"You're taking the first step, Rae, and sometimes that's the hardest one. Your mother would be proud of you," I replied, a lightness in my voice I hadn't felt in a while.

She nodded her head and smiled weakly. As I watched her walk towards the bedroom door, her posture seemed different, not quite as burdened. There was a newfound glimmer of resolution in her eyes.

I couldn't help but feel hopeful. Ailing as I was, her shift toward embracing her destiny was like a soothing balm to my own tormented spirit. I took a deep breath, feeling the tightness in my chest, a stark reminder of my mortality and the relentless progression of my disease.

Time was running out for all of us. We had our roles, but was it enough?

Uncertainty hung in the air, thick and palpable, but for now, there was a crack in the door, a sliver of light spilling through.

And sometimes, that's all you need to keep going.

Chapter Sixteen—Rae

Everything felt like a smudged painting, the colors of the ceremonial space bled into each other. I couldn't tell if it was the remnants of the alcohol still in my system or the gravity of what was about to happen. It was strange and uncomfortable, but it was for Aracely. I owed her this, at least.

I hadn't been back here in years, and part of me couldn't help but dwell on the fact that they had all written me off. Even Jack. Yeah, I was the prodigal daughter, and not the kind who's welcomed back with a feast.

I didn't know what to do with my hands. It was an awkward experience, to say the least. My eyes hurt, my heart weighed heavily and my mouth was dry. As dry as cracker dust.

Why had I agreed to this?

Yes, I had walked into the elders' lodge, my heart pounding like a drum. Everything seemed both familiar and foreign. Then my eyes landed on him—Uncle Waya. He looked so much like Dad, only older and somehow more serene. His eyes were deep pools of something I couldn't quite name, wisdom or maybe sorrow, or a mix of both.

"Welcome back, my niece," he greeted me softly.

"Uncle," I stammered, unsure how to feel. "It's been a long time."

"Too long," he agreed, his eyes locked onto mine. "You have come at the right time, Rae. It is not too late. Your daughter needs you. We need you."

I clenched my fists. What I wanted to do was scream at him. Demand answers. *Why did you hate my husband? Why did you reject me? Reject us? And now you want to save my daughter?* But I said none of that. As Jack reminded me on the way here, time was not on our side.

"If I can help Aracely, tell me what needs to be done."

He gestured for me to sit. "The nunnehi are restless, on the move. They're more than legends now; they're a threat. They have emerged in our time and it is a challenge we must meet."

"And?" I asked rather sarcastically. "Isn't this a task for the elders? Why am I here?"

Of course, I knew the answer. They wanted me to look, to see into the spirit realm but what they didn't know was I forgot how to do that. Or rather, I lost the ability to do that.

Why didn't I just tell them the truth? I can't say.

"It must be you, Rae. You know that. They will not see you. You are the Hidden Eyes of our tribe. This task falls to you, niece."

"I-I-I," I managed to stammer. "I mean I haven't been involved in the tribe's work in years. Why can't you see what they're doing?" I shot back, bitterness making my words sharper than I'd intended. "You're the elders, isn't that what you're supposed to do?"

He sighed, "We can see, but our vision is limited and they will see us. You, Rae, can do more. You can be our eyes where we cannot see. You are hidden from them." Waya sat down next to me, "Our lineage is strong; you are the last in the female line until Aracely takes up the mantle."

I swallowed hard. "I'm scared, Uncle."

"You should be scared. Aracely's ancestry has stirred the nunnehi. She has inadvertently drawn them back to this realm. The blood in your veins, and her veins, it is powerful. They remember it and are drawn to it."

I didn't know what to say. I felt anything but powerful. "I will fail you again, uncle. As I always have. I am afraid. Afraid for Aracely. For me. For everyone."

"Fear doesn't make you weak, Rae. Fear can lend you strength if you do not allow it to conquer you. Draw on it. You must see what the nunnehi are doing. We must know what they want. Even after all these generations, we cannot understand what they want. What promises Keta made. We must know and we must know how to protect Aracely and all of our people."

I felt his words dig deep, somewhere primal, somewhere pure. For the first time in a very long time, I felt like I had a purpose.

"Okay," I finally said, the word heavy but freeing. "I'll do it. I'll see for you, if I can. I warn you, I warn you all that I have not used this power in over a decade. It may not work," I added that last bit hesitantly, but it was better to be honest than not.

He nodded, something like pride glinting in his eyes. "Forgive me, Rae. I was a foolish man. Too proud. I should not have pushed you away, or Ty

Burkhalter, or your daughter. I was wrong. Please forgive me. Forgive us."

That broke me. I thought I would cry, weep, scream, or shout, but I did none of those things. Instead, I experienced a strange sort of breaking. Like a sort of eggshell cracked off my mind, soul and body. I'd been imprisoned by their rejection and my own response to that. And I hadn't even known it.

I understood then. This was bigger than me, bigger than any fear I had. I had to do this for Aracely, for my tribe, and maybe even for myself.

"You won't be alone," Jack said, stepping forward. "I'll be beside you."

My uncle's face darkened. "It's dangerous for others to step into that realm, Jack. Especially in your condition. This is a job for a seer."

"I won't let her go alone. Besides, I am dying already. They will know and I will be protected," Jack insisted as he smiled at me. Was he suggesting that I would protect him?

And so, it was decided.

I had spent years running away from this part of me, but now I had to embrace it. I took a deep breath, each molecule of air filled with the scent of sage and the musty earth. I was terrified, but if it meant saving Aracely, I would step into that spirit world. And somehow, knowing Jack would be beside me made the unimaginable seem possible.

As I sat there, waiting for the ritual to begin, a flicker of hope lit up inside me. But then, a daunting thought settled in—could we, a group of flawed humans, possibly stand a chance against the ancient spirits known as the nunnehi?

The room was filled with the aroma of cedar and sage, their scents mingling in the air as though to forge a protective barrier.

Tribal fabrics with intricate patterns adorned the walls, and the floor beneath us was a worn, warm wood that had seen countless ceremonies and rites. I sat on the floor, my legs crossed, feeling the grainy texture of the fabric cushion beneath me. I didn't remember it being this soft.

In front of me, my uncle was arranging ceremonial items on an intricately designed mat: feathers, a leather pouch filled with herbs, and a small clay pot containing a mysterious liquid that emitted a faint, spicy scent. Once I knew what it all meant.

Though my skin was tingling with a mix of fear and alcohol withdrawal, I felt a surprising calm wash over me.

It was as though the very walls of the space were whispering, comforting me, reminding me that I had returned to a place of unconditional love and acceptance. And as I looked at my uncle's reassuring face, I realized that I would indeed do whatever I had to, that the responsibility—and the power—to save Aracely also rested with me.

As my uncle finished arranging the ceremonial items, he moved toward me and rested his hands on my shoulders. The weight of his touch was firm, grounding, as if he were transferring some ancient strength into me.

"We are glad to have you back, my niece," he said, his voice textured like worn leather, but kind. "You are welcome here, always."

I nodded; my throat suddenly tight. "Thank you, Uncle," I managed to say. It felt like both too much and not nearly enough, but words were all I had. Words, and the newfound resolve that brimmed within me. I would venture into the unknown, confront whatever needed to be confronted.

Tears welled in my eyes, blurring my vision. The room seemed to tighten around me, as if the walls were closing in to whisper the ancient truths I'd tried to shut out for so long. My heart pounded in my chest, the rhythm echoing the spiritual drumming I'd grown up with but had turned away from.

Waya's voice took on the tone of an elder, a master of the ritual. Thus he began the ceremony with the proclamation. "The tribe summons you," he continued. "Your daughter needs you. And Rae," he paused, gripping my shoulders a bit tighter, "you need you. Come back to who you are. Come back, Wandering Feather. Come back to who you are and to the place you belong."

In that moment, an even deeper breaking occurred. I wept with abandon. Years of regret, years of lost time and opportunities, seemed to flood out, replaced by a sense of purpose and belonging that I hadn't felt in ages. It was as though my spirit was finally aligning with my physical being, mending the fractured pieces of my identity.

"Yes, I am she. I am Wandering Feather, the one with the Hidden Eyes," I whispered, the word a commitment, a pledge to honor the lineage that flowed through my veins. "I'll go back. I will see."

"Step onto the path, Wandering Feather. Step on to the path in your mind's eye and see."

As he spoke, my heart swelled with a mix of dread and anticipation. But overriding it all was a feeling of rightness, as if I had finally stepped onto the path I was always meant to walk. Again, I walked the path of the Unseen. And though fear still lurked in the shadowy corners of my mind, I knew I would face whatever lay ahead. I had to. There was simply too much at stake.

I felt Jack's presence beside me although I did not open my eyes. His soul felt peaceful, calm and strong. Stronger than mine.

"The nunnehi will not harm you. You can see what they're doing, why they have returned. Aracely's blood drew them, but they want something more. They always want something more," Jack whispered to me. The air was heavy with the scent of burning herbs, mingling with the earthiness of wet soil and the heady aroma of cedarwood.

"I'm terrified," I confessed, my voice a shaky whisper. The room itself seemed to be pulsing, as if it were a living, breathing entity, attuned to the urgency of the mission ahead.

Jack spoke again in a whisper, "Remember that your lineage protects you. You are a seer, and you have the strength to go where others cannot. It is your right, written into your blood. I am with you."

Taking a deep breath to steady my trembling hands and racing heart, I nodded. "Alright, let's do this."

Uncle Waya began to chant, his voice low and rhythmic, like the ancient heartbeat of our people. As he chanted, I felt myself slipping away, descending into a different plane of existence. The other elders chanted along with him and soon the rhythm became my footsteps and I traveled far and deep.

In the spirit world, I was met with an expanse of shadow and mist, an ethereal landscape that seemed both foreign and familiar. And then I saw them—*nunnehi*, shadow spirits, neither fully here nor there, lingering between worlds. They moved gracefully yet urgently, assembling in a formation that I couldn't quite understand.

Stand behind me, Jack! I will hide you!

My eyes widened as I realized that they were preparing for something, something big and possibly ominous.

As I concentrated harder, images began to flood my senses—flashes of the tribe, of Aracely, of a great disturbance in the balance between our world and theirs.

It was happening! I did it! I made my way back! The colors were sharper, more vivid than anything I'd ever seen. But the beauty was tainted by a looming darkness, a swirling mass of malevolence on the horizon.

The nunnehi. Their shapes twisted, like distorted shadows, and I could feel their hatred pulsing like a poisonous fog. They were gathering something—souls.

Souls of the dead, writhing in torment, their faces contorted in agony. Ancient dead, more recent dead. White, Cherokee, it mattered not to the nunnehi. Anything with a soul was to be gathered by them. Their power depended on their mastery of the dead.

A cold shiver ran down my spine. These spirits were being prepared for war, a war against us—

against the elders, Aracely and the remaining Cherokee. Beyond that, who could say?

Despair washed over me, heavy and thick. We couldn't fight this, could we?

Then something miraculous happened. A soft, ethereal light broke through the inky darkness, and sacred dancers emerged, their bodies glowing in celestial radiance. These were the spirits of our ancestors, the keepers of our sacred traditions. They danced in intricate patterns, their moves a blend of beauty and deadly skill.

I heard Jack gasp beside me. *He saw them too! I'd almost forgotten he was with me.*

As the ghosts of the sacred dancers moved closer, the dark spirits recoiled, their hisses echoing in the spiritual plane.

The sacred dancers faced me, and I felt an immense power surge through me. It was as if they were telling me, telling all of us, that we were not alone. That we had a fighting chance.

With a jolt, I was back in the cabin, gasping for air. *Oh no! Just as I was about to delve deeper!*

Yes, the tug at the core of my being, pulled me back to the physical world. The transition jarring, as if I had been yanked through a vortex of time and space. Uncle Waya and the Elders ceased their chanting, looking at me with eyes full of questions.

"We are not alone," I said, my voice steadier than I felt. "The sacred dancers will fight with us. We have a chance." I glanced at Jack who suddenly appeared a weak and frail man. Not how he usually appeared to me. He put a hand on my shoulder and nodded his head in thanks and appreciation. Maybe I was seeing things, but I could see Death standing behind him.

He would died soon.

Relief washed over their faces, but it was laced with gravity. We were still on the brink, but at least now, we had hope. And sometimes, hope is all you need to turn the tide. Uncle and the elders staring at me, their faces etched with concern and anticipation.

"What else did you see?" Uncle urged.

"They want worship and blood," I said, my voice laced with newfound resolve. "I have seen the nunnehi. They have enslaved the souls of the dead that rest on that land. Enslaved them for their evil purpose."

My heart was pounding, not just with fear, but also with a profound sense of purpose. I was the seer. I had to guide my tribe, protect my family, and maybe, just maybe, save us all.

"But as I said, the sacred dancers of old, have not been captured and they have come for the fight. They will guide you. Guide us." And with that, the elders broke out in whoops of celebration. Many of us smiled, but there was a solemnity that could not be shaken.

I sat there pondering everything that had happened. Love, acceptance, destiny—they had all converged in a single, overwhelming moment, forging my path forward.

My eyes met Jack's, and in that gaze, I saw a glimmer of hope. It was faint but potent.

Yet, as hopeful as it was, a cloud of doubt loomed on the horizon of my thoughts. Were we, a makeshift group of modern-day warriors bound by blood and destiny, truly enough to face the ancient spirits that had awakened?

Jack must have sensed my inner turmoil. "We are not alone. We will find a way. This time, we will win." And so, fortified by a strange blend of love, duty, and fear, we prepared for what lay ahead, the tension of uncertainty hanging heavy in the air.

Would we be the heroes of our own story, or merely characters in a tragedy written long before our time?

It was a question that none of us could answer.

But one thing was certain—we would find out soon enough.

Chapter Seventeen—Aracely

I shot up, gasping for air as if I'd been underwater for too long. Sweat clung to my skin and my heart pounded like a drum in my chest. The nightmare had felt so real, so vivid. I looked around, struggling to separate the horrifying images in my dream from the reality of the room.

Oh, that's right. I fell asleep in Red Sky's bed. We'd been talking and then...

Red Sky was beside me, his eyes blinking open, immediately alert. "Aracely, what's wrong? You look terrified." I rubbed at my eyes, still shocked at my own behavior. I'd actually slept in a near stranger's bed.

At least we kept our clothes on. I mean, we hadn't even kissed. Truth be told, I would not have said no if he'd tried. The kissing part at any rate.

My breath was still coming in short, shaky gasps. "I had a dream, a terrible dream. I was Mrs. Dooley; I think her name was Ellen. No, it was Eliza, I'm not sure. But the shadows—they invaded the home and... they killed the children, Red Sky. Slashed them to death. They demanded innocent blood!"

His eyes widened, a mix of disbelief and concern crossing his face. "Let's look this up. Maybe there's something in the historical records that can help us understand what you saw."

Red Sky gently swung his legs over the side of the bed, giving me a quick, reassuring glance before heading over to the computer desk. I wrapped the blanket around myself, still feeling a shiver of unease. This was the bed Red Sky slept in every night, yet we had only lain beside each other, a respectful distance keeping us apart. The intimacy we shared was emotional, not physical, at least not yet.

My heart was still racing, but the rational part of me hoped that a logical explanation could dull the sharp edges of my fear. We turned to his computer, diving into a world of digital archives and old records, searching for a piece of the puzzle that would make sense of my nightmare. I could see by the many desktop folders on his computer that he'd already created while researching my place.

He started typing, his fingers moving swiftly over the keys as he pulled up a search engine. I hesitated for a moment, then joined him, sitting on the edge of the desk.

Our eyes met, and in that moment, a silent understanding passed between us. This was bigger than any hesitation or awkwardness we might have felt.

"I found something," he said, finally breaking the silence. His eyes were scanning an old newspaper article on the screen. "Mrs. Eliza Dooley, a woman who lived here over a century ago. It says here that she and her children were found murdered in their home. Her husband, Mr. Dooley, killed them and himself after losing his home in a poker game to Mr. Southland. It looks like it was quite the scandal."

My stomach churned at his words, and I felt the color drain from my face. "Southland? That's where the Dooleys lived? That's what I saw, Red Sky. It's exactly what I saw in my dream, but it wasn't him. He did not kill those children. I can't say he didn't kill his wife, or himself, but I saw the shadows. The ones...I don't want to say their name. They did it. They killed the children."

His gaze moved from the screen to meet mine. "We have to figure out what this means, Aracely.

They want innocent blood; that much is clear. But why show this to you, why now?"

"I don't know," I admitted, my voice trembling. "But I have to go back. I can't explain it, but I feel such an urgency. That's my home. I can see it like it should be. I know that it's meant to be something wonderful. God, what have I done? I spent all my money, sunk it into that house. I really believed I could make it beautiful."

Red Sky sighed, his face etched with conflict. "You can still make that happen, Aracely. Maybe, just maybe, the reason you bought the land is more nuanced than that. That land used to belong to the Cherokee. Now it does again."

"So you say," I said as I wrapped the blanket even more tightly around my shoulders. "Red Sky, I can't wait. Something terrible is going to happen, I can feel it. I need to be there. It's my fault. I know it is. If I hadn't bought the land, if I hadn't bought the house, they wouldn't have woken up. I can see that now."

For a long moment, he looked at me, his eyes searching mine as if looking for answers. He knew the truth and so did I. The nunnehi had returned because of me. Because once again,

Cherokee blood walked the land. Apparently even a half blood was enough to summon them.

"What am I going to do?"

Finally, he nodded. "Okay, Aracely. I'll take you there. We'll go back."

A torrent of relief washed over me as Red Sky agreed. It was as though a heavy weight had lifted off my shoulders, even if just slightly. Why? I couldn't say. It wasn't like I knew what I was going to do. Almost immediately, that relief was tinged with apprehension. The urgency I felt wasn't just a nagging thought; it was a pulsing, living thing inside me, as tangible as the air we breathed.

Red Sky seemed to sense my internal struggle. He rose from his chair and took a step towards me. "We'll need to be prepared, in every way possible. Grandfather has some ancient protections—charms and incantations. Let's not forget the pouches he gave us already. I'll gather what else I can and leave him a note."

I nodded, eager for any plan that sounded like it could work. "What can I do?"

"Search for anything related to the Dooley murders," he said, returning to the computer and pulling up another window. "There must be something in that dream that could help us. If we're going, we're leaving as soon as possible."

I could almost hear what he didn't say. *Before we change our minds.*

My fingers trembled as I took the mouse from him, scrolling through digital archives of old newspapers, history forums, and even some paranormal websites. Each click felt like a step closer to the unknown, a journey we were about to embark upon, fueled by a dream—or perhaps a nightmare.

As Red Sky gathered some belongings in a duffel bag—clothes, a first-aid kit, and a few mysterious pouches I assumed were filled with traditional Cherokee protections—I couldn't help but wonder. Were we heading into a trap, or were we the only ones who could stop whatever horror was unfolding?

But deep down, I knew we had no choice. The nightmare had chosen me, for reasons I couldn't fathom. And whatever awaited us, we would face it—together.

My heart was still pounding from the gruesome images of my dream as Red Sky zipped up his duffel bag, his face focused but clearly weighed down by the gravity of our situation. He looked up and met my eyes.

"Whatever it is, whatever those shadows want, we can't let them get it. We must protect those who can't protect themselves. We must find a way to send them back."

His words reverberated in my soul, giving voice to the urgency that had taken hold of me. My eyes watered, but I fought back tears. This wasn't the time for emotional breakdowns. It was the time for action.

"I cannot in good conscience sell Southland to someone else. I can't pass that place on to others. Not now that the nunnehi are back. The former owners reported nominal paranormal activity during their haunted house shows, but this...this isn't the same thing. These aren't merely troublesome ghosts."

Red Sky walked over to me and took my hands, pulling me close. "You're right. You can't do that. You said you felt an urgency, right? That's your spirit telling you we need to intervene and I trust that."

"Why? You hardly know me? You don't know anything about me."

"Don't I? I know enough." He leaned closer to me and I thought for a moment we would kiss, but he pulled back. "We better go."

I nodded and tried to hide my emotions. At least I did find strength in his words. "Okay, then what's the next move?"

"We go back to Southland. Grandfather wants us to wait, but the signs can't be ignored."

At his words, the room seemed to darken, the shadows on the walls growing more ominous, as if the spirits were listening, knowing we were coming for them. But for the first time since this nightmare began, I felt a glimmer of hope.

With Red Sky by my side, armed with ancient wisdom and modern knowledge, maybe—just maybe—we had a fighting chance.

With a deep breath, we stepped out of the cabin, closing the door behind us. But as it latched shut, a haunting thought crossed my mind—were we closing the door on our past, or opening a gateway to a future filled with unimaginable perils?

Either way, there was no turning back.

Chapter Eighteen—Red Sky

As I packed the last of our supplies into the trunk of my car, I felt the air around me shift, like the atmosphere was suddenly heavier. I turned around to see Grandfather Jack standing there, his expression unreadable, but intense. How had he pulled up and I hadn't heard him and his old truck? I must have been lost in my thoughts.

The moment our eyes met, I knew he sensed it too—the urgency, the invisible pull towards Southland.

"Grandfather," I greeted, trying to keep my voice steady. "We're heading to Southland. Something's calling to Aracely—they came to her in a dream, and I can't ignore it any longer."

His eyes narrowed, not in suspicion but in calculation, as if he were piecing together fragments of a much larger puzzle. "I figured as much," he finally said, his voice tinged with a gravity that sent chills down my spine. "The land's spirit is restless, its call seeping even into dreams. And now, it has reached Aracely."

"Yes, and it's urgent," I pressed, my grip tightening on the truck's tailgate. "We have to go, Grandfather."

He took a deep breath, as if drawing the weight of our ancestral history into his lungs. "Then I'll go with you. And so will the elders. The nunnehi are restless, and their thirst for innocent blood is a debt that will be called in. We must face them, as a tribe, and as the last carriers of our ancient lineage."

The word 'nunnehi' hung in the air between us like a dark omen. Evil spirits of another realm, demanding a terrible price. My heart pounded in my chest, but in that moment, I knew we were on a path from which there was no turning back.

We were back inside the cabin, hurriedly gathering the remaining necessities for the journey, when Aracely hesitated and approached Grandfather Jack. I could see her fighting to find the right words, her eyes searching his as if trying to probe the depths of the ocean.

"Jack," she began, her voice laced with an unsettling blend of certainty and dread, "In my dream, it wasn't the Dooley father who killed those children. It was the spirits. The nunnehi."

For a split second, I thought I saw Grandfather's face blanch, a ripple of raw emotion that he quickly concealed. But then he looked at Aracely—really looked at her—and nodded gravely.

"You've been touched by the spirit world, young one," he murmured. "Your vision is a warning, a prophecy. The evil has not just awoken; it's on the move. It's not content with haunting the margins of our world anymore. It wants to invade it."

A shiver ran down my spine. Even though we had been preparing for this, hearing Grandfather articulate it sent the reality crashing down on me. This wasn't just a mythical story or a childhood fable. It was real, and it was happening now.

"I will call the elders," Grandfather declared, snapping me out of my thoughts. "We'll all go to Southland. The battle we've feared is upon us. We must all be prepared."

As he spoke those words, my stomach twisted into knots. But there was also a strange sense of resolve, of destiny. We were plunging into a battle that had been generations in the making. As the last of our ancient lineage, this was a fight we wouldn't run from.

Grandfather's truck's engine rattled like an old man's cough as we navigated the labyrinthine back roads to Southland. He insisted on driving and I didn't argue with him. Each bump we hit resonated through the vehicle, echoing in the worn-out cabin that smelled of sun-aged leather and the rich tobacco of Grandfather's pipe. The exterior creaked and groaned, almost as if the vehicle itself were wary of what lay ahead.

Limbs from the dense foliage lining the road slapped against the sides of the truck with each turn, like hands reaching out to either ward us off or pull us in deeper—I couldn't decide which. It added an eerie percussive rhythm to our journey, each thwack punctuating Grandfather's stern directives.

"Before the last rays of the sun dip below the horizon, we must be ready," Grandfather said, his eyes narrow and locked onto the twisting road. "The veil between worlds is thinnest in the forest, in a clearing only known to our people. That's our battleground."

I glanced at Aracely, and for a moment, our eyes met. It was fleeting but electric, like the brief touch of two live wires. She was anxious, I could tell, but the vulnerability in her eyes beckoned me closer to her. I reached over and clasped her hand, interlocking our fingers. She squeezed back—a silent vow between us that spoke louder than any words could.

The truck rumbled on, drawing us nearer to the unknown. Despite the impending confrontation with the nunnehi, I felt the corners of my mouth twitch into a small, defiant smile. Grandfather's guidance, the call of the ancestral lands, and the inexplicable connection I felt with Aracely—it all swirled together into a potent blend of hope and determination.

As we drove deeper into the shadow-draped woods, I felt not just the weight of our looming battle, but also the birth of something new between Aracely and me.

With every mile that rolled under us, I couldn't shake the feeling that we were driving not only toward a fight for our survival, but also to a defining moment in our intertwined destinies.

In the rearview mirror, I noticed the others. One by one, other vehicles emerged, falling in line behind us. A wash of relief surged through me—

it was the elders, summoned by Grandfather to join the fight.

Seized by a newfound sense of purpose, Grandfather and I broke into a victory song—an old Cherokee anthem that had been sung for generations. It began softly, our voices raw but strong, invoking the spirits of warriors and shamans long passed.

I saw Grandfather's eyes water as he sang, but I knew they weren't tears of sadness. They were tears of pride, defiance, and a deep love for his people.

I glanced at Aracely, and what I saw in her eyes took my breath away.

Her lips were slightly parted as she listened to our song, trying to catch the melody, the rhythm, the heart of it all. She may not have known the words, but I saw her humming along, trying to match the rise and fall of our voices.

At that moment, I was struck by a revelation as powerful as a thunderbolt descending from the sky. *I never loved Susan.* What I felt for Susan was a rain shower, quick and brief, but what I felt for Aracely would be a storm, magnificent and all-encompassing.

This I knew, but how, I could not say.

Our voices rose higher, blending into a harmonious battle cry that seemed to awaken the spirits of the forest. The looming darkness would not stand a chance against our light.

We were armed not just with ancient rituals and legends, but with something even more potent— a love that could defy time, space, and even the ethereal veil separating us from the spirit world.

That moment, singing together on our journey toward an uncertain fate, was when I knew: we could face the nunnehi, and anything else that came our way. We had the wisdom of our ancestors, the courage of warriors, and a love that was destined to transcend realms.

We were ready. Or so I believed.

As our voices reached a crescendo, the truck suddenly jerked, as if jolted by an invisible hand. The truck sputtered and for a split second, a wash of darkness came out of nowhere and threatened to swallow us whole. Grandfather slammed his foot on the brakes, and we skidded to a jarring halt.

The cars behind us also stopped. We waited; nobody left their vehicles. No one honked their horns or dared to make a move.

"We're not alone," Grandfather murmured, his eyes narrowed as he scanned the darkness around us.

I felt it too—a creeping sensation at the back of my neck, a cold breath that wasn't there a moment ago. It was as if the forest itself had paused to listen, its usual sounds replaced by an eerie, almost human-like whisper that rustled the leaves and sent a shiver down my spine.

Aracely clutched my arm tightly, her eyes wide with a mixture of fear and awe. "Did you hear that?" she whispered.

Before I could answer, a ghostly wind rushed through the trees, and for a fleeting moment, I thought I saw shadowy figures darting between the trunks, their eyes glowing like hot coals in the dark.

"Even in the daylight. They're watching us," Grandfather said, his voice tinged with a solemnity I'd never heard before. "The nunnehi are close. They know we're coming."

Our eyes met, a silent understanding passing between us. The real battle was just beginning, and the stakes were higher than we'd ever imagined.

With that thought etched into our hearts, Grandfather put the car in drive again.

Slowly, we began to move, leading the convoy of elders behind us, each of us silently praying that the ancient spirits would truly be on our side when the final confrontation came.

This was a darkness that no man or woman living had ever seen.

And it wanted to claim all of us.

Chapter Nineteen—Aracely

We finally arrived at Southland, the convoy of cars pulling off the dirt road and into the expansive clearing that held so much history for the tribe. The air felt thick, almost suffocating, as if the land itself was holding its breath in anticipation of what was to come.

 My eyes scanned the faces of the elders who had joined us, their expressions etched with a mix of determination and solemnity. But it was another face that caught me off guard—a face I had not expected to see, yet there she was--my mother, Rae.

"Aracely," she called out softly as she walked towards me. Her eyes looked different; they held a spark I had never seen before, or maybe I had just forgotten it was ever there. The weight of a lifetime stretched between us in those few steps it took for her to reach me.

She pulled me to the side, away from the prying eyes and ears. "I know a single moment can't make up for a lifetime of wrongs, but I'm trying, sweetheart," she said, her voice trembling but full of an earnestness I'd never heard before. "Please, let me help you."

For a split second, all the pain and resentment welled up inside me like a dam about to burst. But then I looked into her eyes, really looked, and saw the mother who had carried me, who had once sung lullabies to put me to sleep. And in that fragile moment, my walls began to crumble.

I didn't know if a lifetime of hurt could be mended, if the gaping voids could ever be filled, but as I looked at her, I felt something I hadn't felt in years--hope.

I whispered, finally allowing myself to say the word I'd kept locked away for so long. "Let's do this together."

As the words left my lips, I felt the air grow still around us, a quiet heaviness settling in like a storm cloud. A part of me couldn't help but question it all, question her. How could I trust her? She'd failed me so many times. Lied to me so many times.

I quit drinking, Aracely.

I'm sober, Aracely.

"Are you sure you want to do this?" I asked, my voice tinged with skepticism. "You've always said you didn't want to see anymore. That you hated being a visionary. I have to believe that's why you are here."

She looked down for a moment, her eyes clouded with a mixture of shame and contemplation. When she finally looked up, her gaze met mine with an intensity that startled me.

"You're right," she admitted, "I did say those things. I said a lot of things that I didn't mean, things that should never have been spoken. But sometimes life has a way of showing you what a fool you are, Aracely. I am a fool. I have been one. I must admit that I didn't always know what I wanted, or what I was meant for." I noticed her hands shaking, a clear sign that she needed a drink. Did she mean it this time?

Tears flowed down my mother's face. "I blamed others for your father leaving, but it was me. It was my fault. I chose the coward's way. Forgive me, Aracely. Someday, please. Forgive me."

My eyes watered too, but I refused to collapse again. "But you hate them, Mom. How many times did you tell me that?" I asked, thinking of the countless stories she'd told me about the tribe, about the burdens and betrayals she felt.

Rae sighed deeply; her eyes filled with an emotion I couldn't quite place. "Hate is a heavy burden to carry, Aracely. And I've been carrying it for a long time. But I don't want that for you, and I don't want it for myself anymore."

My breath caught in my throat. The walls around my heart wavered for a moment, and I realized that perhaps we were more alike than I had ever allowed myself to admit. Both of us were struggling with the legacy of our past, and the weight of decisions that were never truly ours to make.

She reached out and took my hand, her grip warm and firm. "I can't undo the past, but I can fight for our future. If you'll let me stand beside you."

I looked at her shaky, sweaty hand holding mine, then back up into her eyes. She continued her confession and said words I never expected to hear.

As we stood there, hands still intertwined, Mom seemed to hesitate, her eyes searching mine for something I couldn't quite define. Then, taking a deep breath as if summoning courage from the very air, she spoke.

"Aracely, I need to say something I should've said long ago," she began, her voice tinged with regret. "I should never have called you names. You are not a 'half-breed,' daughter. You are Cherokee, as I am."

The words landed heavily between us, like a long overdue apology. For a moment, I couldn't speak. My throat tightened, and I felt an unexpected rush of emotions. Anger, relief, and something else—something that felt a lot like forgiveness.

I looked up to meet her eyes, searching for the sincerity I so desperately wanted to see. And there it was. The pain and regret that filled her gaze made the apology real.

"Thank you, Mom," I finally managed to say, my voice barely above a whisper. "That means more to me than you'll ever know."

She nodded, her eyes shining with unshed tears. "Let's make this right, Aracely. For us, for our tribe, for everyone we've lost and everyone we could still save."

"I'm with you," I said, squeezing her hand one last time before we turned to rejoin the others.

Our feet may have been walking on the same broken soil of our ancestors, but for the first time in a long time, it felt like our souls were moving in the same direction too.

We all gathered around the hood of Grandfather Jack's worn-out truck, its rusty frame serving as a makeshift altar. A moment of stillness settled over us, as if the forest itself had hushed its whispering leaves to listen. Uncle Waya stepped forward, his eyes somber but steadfast.

"We are here to face a darkness that threatens to consume us," he began, his voice cutting through the chilling air. "Our tribe's visionary, Rae, has seen into the spirit world. She's seen the nunnehi and the souls and the darkness they're gathering. But she has also seen hope—the spirits of the sacred dancers."

A collective murmur went through the crowd, eyes widening in a mix of dread and awe. Mom stood next to me, her eyes meeting mine for just a second, but in that moment, I saw an unspoken promise.

"Take these amulets, wear them close to your hearts," Waya continued, gesturing towards a basket filled with small, intricately crafted talismans. "They carry the essence of our ancestors, the power to protect."

One by one, we reached into the basket, picking out the amulets and wearing them around our necks. It was a small but symbolic gesture, binding us together as one tribe, one family, facing an unimaginable horror.

Next came the paint. We took turns applying it onto each other's faces and arms, the vibrant colors feeling like war paint for the soul. Words of encouragement were whispered, passed like sacred offerings from one to another.

And then there was Red Sky. We found ourselves standing next to each other, away from the rest for just a moment. He looked into my eyes, took my hand and squeezed it gently. He touched my face with the paint, making two streaks, one under each of my eyes.

"You are no less a warrior than anyone here. We're going to get through this," he whispered, as if saying it out loud would seal it as a promise between us and the universe.

"I know," I whispered back, my eyes meeting his. It was a simple exchange, but it was everything. We released hands and I avoided meeting my mother's curious gaze.

As we rejoined the group, I felt a new weight on my shoulders—not just of dread or fear, but of purpose, of unity, of a destiny we were all sharing. I looked around at the faces of my tribe—my family—I realized that we were already fighting back. And that gave me the courage to face whatever lay ahead.

We were a circle unbroken, each of us a crucial link. I looked up into the looming sky, clouded but unyielding, as if daring the darkness to come and find us.

And in that moment, it felt like we were all speaking a silent vow—to protect, to love, to fight.

And to hope.

We set off, our footsteps mingling with the chorus of forest creatures who called the woods their home. It was already growing dark, unnaturally so. The path ahead was lit only by the revealing patches of sunlight through dense foliage and imposing trees that stretched up to the sky like ancient guardians.

Waya led the way, his pace firm but measured, followed closely by Grandfather Jack. Behind them walked Sharon Two-Bears, her shamanistic beads clicking softly, and Ruth Clearwater, her stoic face betraying no emotion. I did not really know these great men and women but I was proud to be walking with them today. There were many more whose names escaped me.

Every so often, an unsettling sound would rupture the silence—a rustling in the trees, a distant howl, or worse, a laughter-like murmur that seemed to come from nowhere and everywhere at once.

As we moved deeper, a strange fog began to seep between the trees, twisting and turning like ethereal snakes. It swirled around our legs, our faces, making it difficult to see the path ahead, let alone each other.

The fog was a trick, I knew that much. It was the nunnehi's doing, a spectral ruse meant to disorient us, to lead us astray from our sacred destination.

"Stick together!" Waya shouted through the thickening mist; his voice tinged with urgency. "Hold hands if you must. Do not stray from the path!"

Then, just when the fog was at its thickest, a new sound emerged—faint at first but growing steadily louder. Drumming. It was rhythmic and hypnotic, like the heartbeat of the forest itself. The beats seemed to come from everywhere, but a direction could be discerned, a kind of magnetic pull.

"We need to follow the drumming!" Asitaga yelled, readjusting the strap of his leather satchel, and pressing on. "They are guiding us!"

Despite the confusion and the disorienting fog, the drumming provided an odd sense of focus, a spiritual compass of sorts. My hand found Red

Sky's, and we gripped each other tightly, as though our lives depended on it. Maybe they did.

The sound guided us forward, each beat resonating deeper within our souls, summoning us toward what lay ahead—a confrontation with the nunnehi, a struggle for our very existence, and perhaps, a glimmer of hope.

As we pressed on, I couldn't shake the feeling that we were not alone, that hidden eyes were watching our every move, gauging our strengths and weaknesses. The air was thick with anticipation, and every shadow that darted across our peripheral vision, every whisper that seemed to echo through the trees, served as a chilling reminder.

The nunnehi were close. And they were waiting.

As we pushed through the final thicket of trees, we emerged into a clearing—a stark, barren circle where not a single blade of grass dared to grow. A natural amphitheater of sorts, encircled by towering trees that seemed to lean in, as though they, too, were curious spectators to the drama that was about to unfold.

Wasting no time, we began gathering sticks, twigs, and larger pieces of wood from the forest floor. Soon, a pile formed in the center of the clearing. My mom and I worked with the others in silence, each lost in his or her own thoughts, but somehow, our movements were synchronized as though guided by an invisible force.

Once the firewood was arranged, Grandfather Jack struck a match, and the fire roared to life, casting an orange glow across our faces and creating dancing shadows on the trees behind us. The men and women gathered in a semi-circle around the flames, some pulling small, leather-wrapped drums from their satchels.

The drumming began, soft at first, but then growing in intensity. The elders picked up the pace, their faces stern with concentration as they sang a melodic chant, their voices blending in an eerie harmony.

The rhythm seemed to penetrate the air, vibrating through the ground beneath us, as if awakening the spirits that resided there.

Just then, the skies above us began to darken. Clouds materialized out of nowhere, obscuring the sky, as if even the moon and stars were reluctant to witness what was about to occur. A sudden gust of wind swept through the clearing, making the fire flicker and sputter, sending sparks into the air like miniature shooting stars.

The forest itself seemed to respond to the growing tension. The trees swayed ominously, and the leaves rustled in agitation.

In that moment, it was as if the very fabric of the natural world was being distorted, stretched to its limit by the sheer force of the opposing energies at play.

I felt a sudden chill, a creeping dread that was almost palpable, like cold fingers running down my spine. I looked around and saw similar expressions on the faces of the others. We were no longer just a group of people in a clearing; we were part of a larger, cosmic battle, the outcome of which was far from certain.

The drumming grew louder still, reaching a feverish pitch. The men's voices rose to match it, filling the air with a primal sound that seemed older than time itself. As I stood there, gripping a piece of firewood as if it were a talisman, I realized that we had crossed a threshold, that there was no turning back.

And then, just as the tension reached its apex, a new sound pierced through the cacophony—a haunting wail that seemed to come from the very bowels of the earth. A bone-chilling cry that was neither human nor animal, but something far more ancient and malevolent.

"They're here," Rae whispered beside me, her voice tinged with both fear and awe. "The nunnehi have come."

As if on cue, the fire flickered one final time before blazing even brighter, casting its glow upon us like a spotlight. We stood there, encircled by darkness, acutely aware that we were not alone.

The nunnehi were close. And the night was far from over.

Chapter Twenty—Jack

The sacred fire raged in the center of the clearing, flames leaping toward the heavens as if trying to pierce the blackness that enveloped us. A darkness, so thick, so malevolent, it seemed to have a life of its own, as it spread like a shroud across the sky and forest.

The others around the circle, my family, my tribe, they all looked as if they were under a spell—mesmerized by the fire, the drumming, and the ceaseless, primal singing that filled the night air.

It was then that I heard it—sounds that were not of this world yet were hauntingly familiar. High-pitched wails and guttural growls seemed to be coming from deep within the forest, the unsettling orchestra of the nunnehi making their presence known.

My spine tingled as I felt a ripple of fear pass through our circle, but we stood our ground. This was our land, our fight, and we had been preparing for this moment for generations.

As the drumming reached a feverish tempo, I began to see them—the sacred dancers. Ethereal, ghost-like figures emerged from the edge of the clearing, moving gracefully yet deliberately toward the fire. They were adorned in traditional regalia, their faces painted in ancient patterns, and their eyes... their eyes glowed with an inner light that was not of this realm.

Just as they promised, the dead had come.

The ghosts of our ancestors, of elders long passed, were there, visible only for an instant when viewed directly. Yet when I shifted my gaze just so, they became clear as day, standing tall and proud, as if bestowing their strength and wisdom upon us.

I felt a surge of energy, of courage, coursing through me. They were here, they had come for the fight, to stand with us in our most desperate hour. The presence of these sacred dancers and ancestral spirits bolstered our resolve, lifting us out of the palpable dread that had begun to take root. Their appearance was a sign, a sign that we could face this ancient evil and prevail.

Yet as uplifting as this vision was, it also carried with it a great weight. The nunnehi had called upon their demonic forces, forces that

threatened to tear the very fabric of our world, and now our ancestors had joined us.
Two ancient powers were converging on this very spot, and the air was thick with tension, as if the earth itself were holding its breath, waiting for the clash that would undoubtedly ensue.

As I looked around at the faces surrounding me—faces filled with a mixture of fear, awe, and resolute determination—I knew one thing: We were united in this struggle, a struggle older than any of us, yet as immediate as the air we were breathing, the earth we were standing upon.

In that moment, as our voices rose in a guttural crescendo and our drums thundered like the heartbeat of the earth, the forest roared back at us, a deafening sound that seemed to shake the very heavens.

The crackling fire and the relentless beat of the drums had become the heartbeat of our circle, our sanctuary amid encroaching darkness. As the ghostly sacred dancers swirled around the fire, my eyes met Rae's for an instant, and I saw her body stiffen, her eyes widen in alarm.

"They're here," she hissed urgently, her voice barely audible over the drumming. "I can see the nunnehi, moving through the trees, getting closer."

I looked at her sharply, my gut knotting with a new surge of anxiety. Rae had the gift—or the curse—of seeing into realms that most could not. If she said they were here, then they were here.

"Keep your eyes closed," I commanded, keeping my voice steady. "Use your spiritual eyes, not your physical ones. If you look at them directly, they'll have power over you."

I watched as Rae nodded and closed her eyes tightly, her expression one of deep concentration. We were in a perilous situation, standing on the precipice between the world of the living and the world of ancient, malevolent beings.

And then it started—a violent whispering. At first, it was almost indistinguishable from the rustling of the trees, but it soon grew louder, more insidious. The sound seemed to come from all directions, swirling around us in a disorienting cacophony.

The whispers spoke in a tongue that was both foreign and intimately known, as though reaching into the depths of our very souls.

I looked around the circle and saw the impact immediately. Several of the elders, their faces twisted in confusion, had begun to sway slightly, as if entranced. Tayanita, a wise man who had been the backbone of our community for years, took a faltering step away from the circle, his eyes clouded and unfocused. Ahawi, our youngest drummer, ceased his drumming, looking disoriented.

"No!" I roared, my voice cutting through the chaos. "Do not listen to them! Stay strong! They're trying to break us, to lure us away one by one!"

As if jolted awake, the errant members shook their heads and returned to their places, their expressions ones of dawning realization and renewed resolve.

"The nunnehi are playing tricks on us," I warned, my voice tinged with the gravity of our situation. "They're using their voices to lead us astray. We have to be stronger than them, we have to stick together."

And we did. United, both in body and spirit, we focused on the drumming, the singing, the fire, and the celestial presence of our ancestors and the sacred dancers. Our circle held fast, impenetrable, even as the whispering continued and the forest around us seemed to pulse with malevolent energy.

But in my heart, I knew this was only the beginning.

The nunnehi would not give up so easily, and neither would we. It was a battle of wills, a battle for the very soul of our people.

The fire flickered and danced, casting eerie shadows on the faces of the elders, the drummers, and the dancers. We were all locked in a collective focus, staving off the malevolence lurking just beyond the firelight.

But something shifted; I felt it before I saw it—a jarring discord in the spiritual fabric of our circle.

My eyes darted to Rae, and my heart sank. She had opened her eyes.

Despite my warnings, despite her own knowledge of the dangers, she had looked. Her eyes were no longer her own; they had taken on an otherworldly glow, a sickening mix of colors that were not natural.

"Stop it!" she screamed, her voice like shattered glass, grating and unnatural. "Stop the drumming, stop the singing! You have no idea what you're doing! Keta made a promise! A promise written in blood!"

Her words carried an ominous weight, laden with a darkness that was not her own. The drumming faltered, the singing wavered, and for a heartbeat, our unified defense was in jeopardy.

"Do not listen to her! That's not Rae speaking!" I shouted, my voice strained with urgency and fear. "Keep drumming, keep singing, for the love of our ancestors, keep going!"

But Rae—or the entity that had taken hold of her—was relentless. She began moving towards the elders, her body convulsing unnaturally, her arms outstretched as if to grasp and tear the very air.

"You will obey me!" she howled, her voice rising to an unholy pitch that made the skin on my arms crawl. "Stop this foolishness now, or you will all perish!"

It was an agonizing spectacle, watching someone I loved being manipulated by a malevolent force beyond comprehension. But I knew what had to be done.

Gathering every ounce of strength, both physical and spiritual, I moved towards her, whispering a Cherokee prayer of exorcism under my breath. With each step, I felt the ancestral spirits rising, their ghostly hands joining mine in a gesture of collective resistance.

"Leave her!" I commanded, my voice booming with a power that was not entirely my own. "You have no place here! Leave her now!"

For a moment, Rae's body stiffened, as if caught in a cosmic tug-of-war. Then, with a scream that tore through the night, she collapsed to the ground.

The entity, the dark force that had overtaken her, seemed to evaporate, dissipating into a cloud of black mist that the wind carried away into the forest.

Rae lay there, panting, her eyes returning to their natural state. But the cost of this battle was etched into every face around the circle. This was a war of attrition, each side testing the other's limits, pushing boundaries, seeking weaknesses.

And as I looked into the eyes of our Elders, our drummers, and our dancers, both living and ancestral, I knew one thing for certain: this was not the end. It was merely a dark prelude to what lay ahead, and we braced ourselves for the final confrontation that was surely coming.

I watched as Aracely rushed to her mother's side, her face etched with terror and love in equal measure. "Close your eyes, Mom! Don't look anymore!" she begged, trying to shield Rae from whatever malevolence that still lingered.

But Rae, her eyes still tinged with the dark influence that had just left her, screamed and clawed at her own daughter. It was a sight that crushed my soul; a mother's love, tainted and twisted by the very darkness we were fighting against.

Reacting instinctively, I grabbed Aracely and pulled her back, away from her struggling mother. "Leave her be, Aracely. She's still fighting it off. You can't help her like this," I said, locking eyes with her.

"But Jack, how do I help her? What do I do?" Aracely's voice was tinged with desperation, her eyes filling with tears.

I held her by the shoulders, grounding myself as I felt the weight of generations upon me. "Sing, Aracely. Lift your voice. That is how you help her. That's how you help all of us. Everyone, sing!"

As if carried by a force larger than us, our voices lifted in unison. The drumming intensified, the elders' chants filling the air with a renewed energy that seemed to dispel the shadows inch by inch. I could see the ancestral spirits rise higher, emboldened by our unity, standing behind each drummer, each singer, fortifying our defense.

And as our voices soared, I noticed the change in Rae. Her body relaxed, her face softened, and the dark glint in her eyes began to fade, replaced by their natural warm hue. Her lips moved silently, as if whispering a prayer, or perhaps a thank you.

In that moment, as our song reached a fervent pitch, I felt it—a tipping point, a crack in the darkness that had encased us. It was as if our collective will, fortified by the spirit of every Cherokee who had come before us, had fractured the impenetrable wall of malevolence.

Yet, I knew we couldn't afford to be complacent. For even as we sang, even as Rae rejoined our circle, even as Aracely's young but powerful voice melded with ours, I felt the ominous presence of the nunnehi retreating, but not vanquished.

The battle was far from over, and it was a harrowing reminder that the line between victory and defeat was perilously thin.
We continued to sing, our voices echoing into the night, shaking the very heavens and earth. And somewhere in that haunting melody was a promise—to fight, to protect, and to reclaim what was rightfully ours.

Peace and life. Peace and life. Those words reverberated through me.

Waya's eyes met mine, and without a word, he began to change the rhythm. The tempo shifted to something slower, each beat more deliberate,

resonating deeper into the soul of the forest—
and our own.

This was not just any song; it was an invocation
to the Great Spirit, a plea for divine intervention
in our darkest hour. This was a powerful song
rarely sang.

The words of the song were as old as the
mountains around us, older than any of us
standing there. I felt them rise up from within,
filling my mouth and spilling into the night air
like sacred smoke.

Every word was a prayer, each phrase a building
block in a bridge to the heavens.

As the rhythm settled into this new, haunting
cadence, I began to see them—the invisible
dancers. They weaved in and out of our circle
with grace, the borders between this world and
the next blurring with each step they took. I
could feel the force of their ancient energy
intertwining with ours, strengthening us for the
battle that raged around and within.

But the nunnehi would not be easily thwarted.
With a hiss that cut through the night, snakes
began to appear within our circle, slithering

menacingly towards us. The very sight of them caused panic, disrupting the unity of our song for a moment.

"Keep singing!" I shouted, my voice reverberating over the frenetic rustle of the snakes. "They are illusions, tests of our resolve! Sing to the Great Spirit!"

Reluctantly, eyes still wide with fear, the circle picked up the song once again. The words were heavier now, each syllable weighed down by the very real threat that loomed over us. Yet we sang, louder and more forcefully than before.

As our voices filled the forest, I felt it—a sudden stillness, as if the world itself was holding its breath. The snakes wavered, their forms flickering like a mirage until they disappeared, vanquished by the power of our unified voices and the invisible dancers who shielded us.

I looked around, locking eyes with Waya, with Rae, with Aracely, and all the Elders. We were still standing, still singing. And though the darkness had not fully retreated, for that moment, it felt like the tiniest crack had appeared in its oppressive wall, letting in a glimmer of something brighter.

The battle was not yet won, but it was a start—a glimmer of hope in the depths of night.

With renewed resolve, we sang on, each word a defiant stand against the shadows, each note a prayer ascending to the Great Spirit who watched over us all. We pled with him to break the unholy contract, to intervene on our behalf.

The forest grew heavier with an almost palpable malevolence as I felt the first touch of the nunnehi against my skin. It was like a chill, a freezing tendril that started wrapping itself around my legs. I could see them now, dark coils rising from the ground like sentient shadows, trying to leech away my will, my focus, my spirit.

For a moment, panic gripped me.

My voice wavered, almost succumbing to the physical and emotional assault. But then I tightened my grip on the drumstick, my fingers white with the effort, and kept my focus laser-sharp on the rhythm, on the words that had been passed down from generation to generation.

This was not just my fight; it was the fight of all those who had come before me, all those who would come after. I would not let them down.

And just when it seemed like the nunnehi would tighten their hold, a figure stepped into view—a spectral shape, but familiar somehow. My heart caught in my throat as I recognized the visage of one of my ancestors, a warrior chief who had led our people through battles of a different kind, long ago. His eyes met mine, filled with a ferocity that time had not dimmed, and he lunged at the shadowy snakes entangling my legs.

What followed was a struggle beyond words, a spiritual combat that seemed to defy the very laws of nature. My ancestor's hands grasped at the shadowy forms, wrestling with them as if he were in a life-and-death struggle with a tangible enemy.

The forest around us seemed to hold its breath, waiting for the outcome of this cosmic battle.

And then, with a final, guttural cry that echoed through the woods and the very chambers of my soul, my ancestor tore the nunnehi away from me, hurling them into the fire where they dissipated into wisps of dark smoke. He gave me one last nod, a silent affirmation that echoed across the centuries, before fading back into the realm from which he had come.

My legs felt lighter, unburdened. But more importantly, my spirit soared. Even as the woods remained a battleground, filled with dangers seen and unseen.

The drumming picked up pace, the singing intensified. The ancestral spirits were with us, and for the first time, I dared to believe that we might yet stand a chance.

I pounded the drum, each beat resonated with the collective spirit of our people, a sudden weight settled over me—a heaviness I couldn't shake.

My bones ached like never before, as if the disease that had long lurked in the background was seizing this moment of weakness to strike. My hands trembled, and for a fleeting moment, I felt my grip slacken on the drumstick.

Then a whisper snaked into my ear, soft but tinged with venom. "You will die a terrible death, old man," it hissed. *The voice of the nunnehi.* My skin crawled, my heart pounded in dread, but I refused to let the voice shatter my resolve.

Just when I felt as if I couldn't go on, as if the weight of centuries and the malice of malevolent spirits would finally crush me, something miraculous happened.

I looked up and saw the night sky transforming, the stars above glowing brighter and shifting into ancient patterns and constellations. Shapes and symbols that told the story of our people, our legends, our battles, and our triumphs. The heavens themselves seemed to be aligning in our favor.

A wave of strength washed over me, as if the very cosmos had infused me with renewed vitality. The ache in my bones lessened, the weariness lifted, and I felt the grip of the disease loosen, if only for this crucial moment. It was as if the universe itself was telling me, telling all of us, that we were not alone—that a force greater than any we could comprehend was with us.

I tightened my grip on the drum and pounded with newfound energy. The sound that erupted was so loud, so powerful, it seemed to reverberate through the very fabric of the universe.

The ancestral spirits cheered, their ethereal forms shimmering with light, and even the nunnehi seemed to pause, as if bewildered by this sudden turn of events.

I knew the battle was far from over, that challenges and possibly tragedies still awaited us. In that singular, defining moment, I felt more alive than I had in years.

But in my heart, I knew my end was near.

So be it. Let Death come.

Chapter Twenty-One—Aracely

My throat was dry, and my voice wavered, but I tried my best to mimic the chant that I'd heard the elders sing. As I sang, I felt a warmth spread through my body, as if the very act of singing was a balm for my soul.

Just then, the fire behind us flared up, casting a warm glow over the clearing. I looked up, and for a moment, my fears subsided. The stars overhead twinkled so brightly, they seemed like a sky full of diamonds, showering us with their celestial light.

But my awe was short-lived.

My eyes widened as a figure suddenly appeared before me—a nunnehi. Facing it was like staring into an abyss, a darkness so deep and complete that it felt as if it could swallow me whole. The contrast between the twinkling stars and the void in front of me was staggering, and for a moment, I felt as if I were standing at the precipice of two worlds, one of light and one of unimaginable darkness.

The nunnehi's form seemed to ripple, as if the boundaries between it and the surrounding night were dissolving. Its voice slid into my thoughts, a chilling whisper that was as enticing as it was terrifying.

Give in, Aracely. Give us your soul and your suffering will end. You can be at peace. Serve us and we shall serve you.

A seductive calm washed over me, tempting me to stop fighting, to let go. But then, I remembered my mother—writhing, struggling against her own darkness. I thought of Jack, standing steadfast despite his weariness, of Red Sky, his eyes always so full of hope. The love and fear for my people snapped me back to reality.

With a renewed strength, I focused on the chant that Red Sky had whispered into my ear. I sang it loudly, defiantly, pouring all the love, all the fear, all the hope I had into each syllable.

The nunnehi recoiled as if struck, its form flickering like a failing light. My song was a blade, sharp and true, cutting through the dark veil that had almost claimed me.

"Aracely, keep singing!" Red Sky's voice broke through, his words a lifeline I eagerly grasped.

With a final note that soared high into the night,
filled with the collective strength of everyone I
loved, the nunnehi before me shattered into
fragments, dissipating into the cold night air.

I had faced the abyss and survived, anchored by
love and fortified by ancestral songs that carried
the wisdom and resilience of generations.

The battle was far from over, but in that
moment, standing at the edge of darkness and
light, I knew we had a fighting chance. And I
wasn't about to give up—not now, not ever.

The forest seemed to ripple, shadows breaking
off and darting like nightmarish figments.

Another nunnehi lunged at me, its form almost
liquid, eyes empty pools of despair. But just as it
was about to reach me, a figure materialized out
of the darkness, a sacred ghost dancer adorned
in ethereal garments that glowed in the night.

My scream was caught in my throat as the ghost
dancer grabbed the lunging nunnehi and, in one
swift motion, hurled it into the raging fire.

The instant they touched the flames, blue sparks
erupted like a torrent of electric rain, scattering

into the inky sky. The fire roared as if in triumph, consuming the evil spirit.

I looked up and saw the stars above us shifting, twinkling brighter, almost as if the heavens were rearranging themselves for this very moment. The celestial dance was a signal—a crack of light in a world of unrelenting darkness.

"Sing, everyone, sing!" Jack's voice reverberated through the night, snapping me out of my trance. "There are more nunnehi coming!"

His warning filled the air, a call to arms that sent ripples through every soul gathered around the fire. It was a reminder that though we had won a small victory, the war was far from over. But for that instant, as the ghost dancers swirled around us and the ancestors' drumbeats pulsed in the depths of our souls, I knew that we stood united.

As I watched, Waya grappled with a shadow, its tendrils curling around his arms and legs snakelike in a dark embrace. Just when I thought he would be consumed, a ghost dancer swept in like a gust of wind, disentangling the shadow from Waya and throwing it into the fire, where it was consumed in a burst of blue flame.

The battle around us was intensifying. Each elder, each warrior, was being tested by these malevolent spirits, the nunnehi relentless in their assault. It was a maelstrom of darkness and light, a clash between ancestral courage and otherworldly malice.

My heart plummeted when I saw my mother, Rae, again convulse, her eyes rolling back once again. Possessed, she lunged at me, arms outstretched as if to push me into the roaring fire.

Time seemed to slow as I fell backward, dangerously close to the flames. In that fleeting moment, our eyes met. I screamed, "I love you, Mom!"

Something in my words broke through. A flicker of recognition flashed in her eyes, the dark veil lifting. Just in time, Red Sky and Jack grabbed my arms, pulling me back from the brink, saving me from tumbling into the hellish blaze.

The spell that had ensnared my mother was shattered, if only for a moment. She looked at me, tears mingling with the ritualistic paint on her face, and I saw her—the real her—emerge from the darkness.

It was as if my words had forged a protective circle around us, one strong enough to banish, even briefly, the malevolent forces that sought to claim us.

Tears streaming down our faces, my mother and I collapsed into each other's arms.

For that one precious moment, the chaos around us seemed to blur into the background. But we couldn't afford to lose focus, not with the battle raging on. We held each other tightly, our voices joining the chant that filled the air, the lifeline that connected us to something greater, something beyond this nightmarish realm.

The very atmosphere changed, as if the forest itself held its breath. The nunnehi charged at the elders again, their numbers seemingly undiminished. And this time, something else stepped into the circle, something far more horrifying—a shadow creature with twisted horns, its form exuding malevolence.

It was unlike anything I had ever seen, and it sent a shiver down my spine, freezing my very soul.

The new entity emanated an aura of dread that seemed to quench the light of our fire. It moved deliberately, cutting through the crowd as if parting water, its eyes—or where eyes should be—fixed on Red Sky.

Red Sky met its gaze, his posture stiffening as if bracing for an impact.

The shadow creature raised its horned head, as though preparing to strike, and in that terrible moment, the air pulsated with an energy so malevolent it felt like the sky would crack open.

The chanting faltered; the rhythm disrupted by the appearance of this new malevolence.

Despite the palpable fear, our eyes met across the circle, a silent understanding exchanged. This was an enemy unlike any we had faced, and it had its sights set on Red Sky. As its dark eyes locked onto him, a chill so profound enveloped us, I felt the night close in, as if trying to swallow us whole.

The tension was unbearable, the dread all-consuming.

We were on the precipice, teetering on the edge of an abyss, and the real battle—the one that would decide everything—was just about to begin.

"Red Sky!" I screamed as I clung to my mother. "No!"

That was all I could think to say as the darkest shadow I'd ever seen began to grow even taller, more muscular and certainly eviller.

And he wanted Red Sky.

Chapter Twenty-Two—Red Sky

As my eyes locked onto the behemoth shadow that loomed before me, an icy shiver raced down my spine. Its darkness was unlike anything I'd ever seen, as if it were woven from the very fabric of nightmares.

My hands trembled, my heart pounded like a war drum in my chest, each beat echoing the grim realization that this was no ordinary enemy. This monstrosity was something far more ancient and more powerful than the nunnehi we'd faced. This was the thing that commanded the nunnehi.

And it had set its sights squarely on me.

For a moment, time seemed to freeze. The firelight flickered ominously, casting grotesque shadows that danced menacingly around us. The chants of the elders became a distant hum, drowned out by the blood roaring in my ears and the chilling whispers that this shadowy figure seemed to send into the very air around it.

In that instant, I understood I was the target, the fulcrum on which the battle would turn. And my soul felt the weight of that responsibility, as heavy and suffocating as the dark cloud that now enveloped us all.

Amidst the chaotic swirl of noise and terror, a sound pierced through, distinct and familiar.

Was it Grandfather shouting? Or was it the strains of a battle song that our ancestors had sung? It was hard to tell in that frenzied moment, but whatever it was, it resonated deep within me, igniting a spark of courage that pushed back against the paralyzing dread.

Just in time, too. The shadowy monster lashed out with a whip made of pure darkness, a weapon so sinister it seemed to absorb the very light around it. My instincts kicked in, and I ducked, feeling the malevolent force whoosh above my head, close enough to send a frigid wind through my hair.

The near miss both terrified and invigorated me. Grandfather's voice—whether in shout or song— had been a lifeline, reminding me that I was not alone, that generations stood behind me. I tightened my grip on the bow I held in my hand, steadied my stance, and braced myself for whatever would come next.

Where had this bow come from? I couldn't say but I instinctively reached for an arrow and found one. I nocked the arrow and aimed it at the beast.

The shadow grinned, and its smile was a horrific display—a mouth filled with flames that flickered like the tongues of some infernal serpent. It sniffed the air, savoring the atmosphere as if tasting our collective fears. "I smell innocence," it rasped, its voice a guttural growl that sent shivers down my spine. "Give her to me, give yourself to me, and I will leave them alone."

In that instant, I realized something had changed. I was the ancient warrior from my vision, the embodiment of my tribe's resilience and courage through the ages. I was here again, facing this monster for a second time.

My heart pounded in my chest, not just with fear but with a newfound resolve.

I stared into the fiery abyss of its mouth, meeting its eyes that were blacker than the darkest night, and thought of Aracely, of Grandfather, of the whole tribe that had rallied for this fateful confrontation.

I couldn't—wouldn't—give in to this monstrosity.

"I will not give anyone to you," I declared, pulling the bowstring taut. "You will leave, but it will be because we've banished you back to the darkness where you belong."

The arrow was steady, and so was my resolve. Whatever happened next, I was ready. I shot the first arrow. It narrowly missed the beast but I grabbed another one.

The battle raged on around me. Elders clashed with shadows, their forms twisting and writhing in a horrific dance. Sacred ghost dancers dashed between us, seizing the dark figures and dragging them into the crackling fire, where they disintegrated into a burst of blue sparks. But the monster before me was different. It stood its ground, unyielding, as if fueled by a malevolent force that defied the sacred.

"You will worship me or I will take what is mine!" it roared, its voice echoing through the forest, bouncing off the trees as if the very land was recoiling in horror. "I have a contract, an agreement made with your ancestors! It is written in your blood—in her blood!"

My blood ran cold at the mention of a contract, a dark deal stretching back through the lineage, a thread of treachery woven into the fabric of our tribe's history.

What had been done? What pact had been sealed in shadows and deceit?

For a moment, my grip on the bow wavered, my fingers trembling with the weight of our collective past. But then I looked around—my eyes locking onto Aracely's terrified face, glancing at Grandfather's stern visage—and my resolve hardened.

"You have no power here," I retorted, my voice rising above the cacophony of battle. "Our ancestors may have erred, but we will set it right. You will not claim what is not yours to take."

The monster snarled, a sound so guttural and vile it seemed to vibrate in the very air around us, distorting reality itself. But I held my ground, my eyes never leaving its face, my fingers gripping the bowstring.

I was Red Sky, the returned warrior. And this—this abomination before me—would not break me. I would not let it break us.

Exhaustion clawed at me like a living thing, a weight pulling down on my limbs, making each arrow I notched feel like a monumental effort. My muscles screamed in protest as I let another arrow fly. It soared through the air, a streak of desperate hope, only to pass right through the monster as if it were a mirage.

A guttural laugh erupted from the creature, taunting me, daring me to surrender to despair.

I could feel the collective fatigue settling over all of us. We were a worn-out, fraying tapestry, and this monster seemed ready to tear us apart at the seams.

Just then, through the haze of weariness and terror, I heard it—a voice, weathered yet strong, cutting through the chaos.

"Sing, Red Sky!" It was my grandfather's voice, as unmistakable as the color of the dawn.

Sing? In the midst of all this?

The idea seemed ludicrous, almost absurd, but there was something in the timbre of Grandfather's voice that left no room for doubt.

He was certain, and that certainty became my lifeline.

Summoning energy from reserves I didn't know I had, I opened my mouth and began to sing. My voice was shaky at first, a mere whisper against the night. But as I sang, something miraculous happened.

My voice grew stronger, surer, and it seemed to meld with the sounds of the others—the chants, the drumming, the night cries of the sacred dancers—as if we were a single organism, a united front against the darkness.

I felt something shift within me, a torrent of newfound strength coursing through my veins. My grip on the bow tightened, my aim steadied. For the first time since this horror began, I felt as if we might have a chance. I could feel it—deep in my bones, deep in the very essence of who I was.

Red Sky. The shaman of his tribe.

The song poured out of me like a river, a torrent of sound that seemed to grow and swell until it filled the entire clearing. As I reached the crescendo, I cast my bow and arrow into the fire beside me. The flames roared higher, a fiery pillar reaching skyward as if answering my call.

That's when the monster let out a soul-chilling roar, a sound so malevolent it shook the very earth beneath us.

Its eyes, those terrible fiery orbs, locked onto me with an expression of pure, undiluted hatred. It was a gaze that promised untold suffering, a gaze I will never forget.

But something incredible happened. Above us, the stars—those same twinkling lights that had been a constant backdrop to our struggle—began to shift and move, like pieces in a cosmic puzzle. They reformed into the shape of a stallion, majestic and awe-inspiring, composed entirely of celestial light.

With a neigh that seemed to shake the heavens, the star-stallion broke from its constellation and streaked down toward us, a blaze of astral fury.

With a powerful kick, it struck the massive monster square in the chest, sending it hurtling backward into the fire.

An explosion ripped through the clearing, a shockwave of light and sound so intense it felt as if the world itself might shatter. The earth beneath us rumbled as the bowels of hell welcomed the creature back. And just like that, the monster was gone, consumed by the flames and the light of the celestial stallion.

The fire, once a symbol of our peril, now seemed to dance in celebration, casting its warm glow upon each one of us. The darkness had been vanquished, at least for now, and in its place was a newfound sense of hope, of unity, of indescribable relief.

As I stood there, panting, my eyes met those of my grandfather, Aracely, and all the brave souls who had stood with us. We had faced the abyss, and we had emerged victorious. But the battle had exacted its toll, and as the adrenaline began to wane, I felt an exhaustion so profound I could barely stand.

Yet, in that moment, tired as I was, I had never felt more alive.

The forest fell eerily silent, the drums that had been the heartbeat of our struggle abruptly stilled. The remaining sacred dancer ghosts turned to us, their ethereal forms glowing softly in the firelight.

One by one, they raised their hands in the universal sign of peace, a final farewell before stepping into the flames. As they did, the fire crackled and popped, sending up sparks that twinkled like stars before disappearing into the night. With their help, we had accomplished what they had not in their lifetimes.

I felt a rush of warmth envelop me as the elders, these venerable men and women who had fought so valiantly beside me, approached. Their eyes met mine, filled not just with relief, but also with something more: recognition, acceptance, even admiration. One by one, they embraced me, and for the first time, they called me "brother."

The weight of that single word was staggering, its implications far-reaching. In that moment, I understood that I was no longer the outsider, the young upstart questioning traditions.

I was their spiritual leader, their shaman, a part of a lineage that stretched back for generations. It was a mantle I had never sought, but one I now accepted with the gravest sense of duty and the greatest of honors.

Finally, my eyes found Aracely's.

She was radiant, her face streaked with the ash and paint and the sweat of battle, yet impossibly beautiful. As she stepped forward, the world seemed to fall away until it was just the two of us, standing there in the glow of the fire.

And then she kissed me, a kiss that tasted of hope and love and endless possibilities, sealing our shared destiny.

The silence of the forest was no longer menacing, but peaceful—a peace hard-won but richly deserved.

As I stood there, surrounded by my newfound family, I realized that this was only the beginning. There were still many challenges to face, many questions to answer, but for now, for this precious moment, we could breathe.

We were alive, and we were free.

Epilogue—Red Sky

My heart sank to my stomach when I found Grandfather Jack sitting against a lone tree, his satchel beside him. It felt as though the earth had shifted beneath my feet. All at once, the noise around me seemed to fade away, leaving only a void filled with sorrow.

I fell to my knees beside him, my body shaking, my eyes blurred with tears.

I let out a deep, agonizing cry, the kind that tears through your very soul. In that moment, the reality of how sick he had been crashed over me like a tidal wave. I'd found out too late. I had been too wrapped up in my own struggles to see the pain he was hiding. And now, it felt like a part of me had been ripped away, leaving a hollow space that nothing could fill.

Grandfather Jack's face, weathered from years of wisdom and challenges, bore the marks of someone who had lived life fully. His eyes were closed now, but in life, they had been a deep, wise brown, like the bark of an ancient oak. His skin, the color of rich earth, was like a living tapestry of our people's history.

A memory surged to the forefront of my mind, filling my senses with the nostalgia of simpler times. I was about ten years old, sitting with Grandfather Jack on the porch of our modest cabin. He was teaching me how to string a traditional Cherokee bow.

"Remember, Red Sky," he said softly, his hands guiding mine, "it's not just about the strength of the wood or the tightness of the string; it's about the spirit you pour into it, the intention behind every move you make."

Here we were, at the end of one journey and perhaps at the start of another.

Grandfather Jack may have taken his last breath, but the lessons he taught me, the love he gave, lived on. I'd been so consumed with being accepted by the tribe, so focused on the immediate challenges, that I had failed to notice the fading strength of the man who had shaped me.

The weight of regret was immense, but so too was my gratitude for the time and teachings he'd shared.

As I sat there, lost in a sea of memories and emotions, the elders approached. Their faces were etched with the lines of wisdom and loss, but their eyes radiated warmth and understanding.

Waya, one of the eldest among them, laid a hand on my shoulder.

"The ancestors have claimed him, Red Sky," he said, his voice echoing with a kind of sacred respect. "He has been called to sit in council with those who walked this land before us. He will be greatly honored. Your grandfather lived as a guide for us all; now he will guide us from the other side."

It was as if a warm blanket of comfort had been laid over me. I looked up and saw Aracely making her way toward me. Her eyes met mine, and I could see her own struggle to reconcile the whirlwind of events we'd been through.

She walked over and knelt beside me, taking my hand as we looked at Grandfather Jack one final time. The elders began to prepare his body for its last journey, placing sage and cedar in his satchel.

"I am here," Aracely whispered.

I took a deep breath, feeling the heaviness of loss entangled with the promise of a new beginning. "Thank you," I replied. We had fought against darkness and prevailed. We had won acceptance and understanding, not just from our tribe but from ourselves.

And as we stood there, surrounded by those who had guided us and those we had yet to guide, I knew that the legacy of Grandfather Jack, and the wisdom of all our ancestors, would continue to light our way.

As the elders delicately arranged Grandfather Jack's body on a traditional blanket, a vehicle pulled up to escort him away. The atmosphere was charged with a blend of sorrow and reverence, each of us aware of the monumental weight of the moment.

My emotions were a storm inside me. Anger, because I hadn't known how sick Grandfather Jack was; and profound gratitude, touched by the tribe's outpouring of love and respect for him. I looked at Waya, who seemed to sense the conflict tearing at me.

"Red Sky," he began, his voice measured, "your grandfather knew what he was doing. He was aware of his condition and chose this path for himself."

"But why?" The question sprang from my lips before I could contain it. "Why didn't he tell me?"

Waya sighed, "As a warrior and a guide, it was his prerogative to choose the manner in which he would cross into the next world. For some, that choice is deeply personal, even private. He didn't want his battle to become yours or overshadow the challenges the tribe had to face. But make no mistake, he loved you deeply and believed in you every step of the way."

As I heard Waya's words, the anger began to dissolve, replaced by a solemn understanding. In his own way, Grandfather Jack had bestowed upon me the highest honor by trusting me to carry on without him, by believing in my ability to lead and grow. It didn't make the loss any easier, but it did offer a different perspective on his choices.

"He was a great warrior but an even greater friend," I murmured, more to myself than anyone else.

"Yes," Waya agreed, nodding slowly, "and now you must be the warrior he knew you could be."

Aracely gently took my hand and squeezed it, grounding me back to the present moment. I looked at her, and for a moment, the weight of everything seemed a little lighter.

As they moved his body, the soft drumming started, low and reverential, carried out by some of the elders who had fought beside us against the nunnehi. It was a tribute not only to Grandfather Jack but to the sacred drummers, those ancestral spirits who'd come to our aid in our time of dire need.

The beats seemed to reverberate in the very core of my being, grounding me, reminding me of the journey, of the battle, of the legacy I now carried forward.

As the drumming continued, Aracely and I stood hand in hand, our hearts beating in sync with the rhythm. It was as if each beat was a word, a message from the ancestors and from

Grandfather Jack himself, telling us to be strong, to love deeply, and to keep the traditions alive.

"Remember this moment," Aracely whispered, her words barely audible over the drums. "This is who you are—who we are. This is what we fought for. And this is what we must continue to protect and honor."

And in that instant, surrounded by my tribe, fortified by their love and their faith, I felt ready to step into the daunting yet sacred role that destiny had set before me.

I felt a sense of profound gratitude, for my love, my tribe, and most of all, for Grandfather Jack, whose spirit would forever guide me through the challenges and triumphs that awaited.

As the last drumbeat reverberated through the hills, fading into the stillness of the afternoon, I felt a strange sense of relief for Grandfather.

Rae was there too. She hugged me and kissed her daughter's cheek. "Your grandfather once told me that our greatest test is how well we walk through the fire," she said, her voice tinged with emotion. "Well, we've walked through it, Red Sky. And we've emerged stronger."

I looked up at the sky, where the sun seemed to shine brighter than I'd ever seen before, as if affirming that the battle we had won was just the first of many victories to come. I thought about Grandfather Jack, about the wisdom he imparted, the love he gave, and the legacy he left behind.

Later that day, after the burial ceremony, Aracely and I looked towards where Grandfather Jack had been laid to rest, and for a brief moment, I could have sworn I saw a shadow, a figure standing there, nodding approvingly at us.

"Thank you, Grandfather," I whispered, my voice carried away by the wind, as we turned and walked back towards our tribe, our family, ready to honor the old ways while forging new paths under the same ancient, watchful stars.

And so, we would step into our future, knowing that the spirits of our past would forever walk with us.

We would need them in the days ahead.

Made in the USA
Middletown, DE
31 March 2024

52376211R00176